THE FRAT WAGON

The Second World War is coming to a...
and the Occupation of German... ...
beginning. Men and women are tasting the
degradation of defeat. Here are th...
experiences and suffering not just o...
Germans but also some of the British ...ps
at a time of great change, painting a
frightening and brutal picture of life i... post-
war Germany.

THE FRAT WAGON

THE FRAT WAGON

by

Charles Whiting

Dales Large Print Books
Long Preston, North Yorkshire,
BD23 4ND, England.

British Library Cataloguing in Publication Data.

Whiting, Charles
     The frat wagon.

     A catalogue record of this book is
     available from the British Library

     ISBN   978-1-84262-608-5 pbk

First published in Great Britain 1954 by Jonathan Cape Ltd.

Published in Large Print 2008 by arrangement with
Eskdale Publishing

Dales Large Print is an imprint of Library Magna Books Ltd.

Printed and bound in Great Britain by
T.J. (International) Ltd., Cornwall, PL28 8RW

CONTENTS

APRIL   9
MAY   45
JUNE   87
JULY   143
AUGUST   178
SEPTEMBER   233

CHAPTER I

APRIL

I had a comrade, a better one you'll never
  find.
The drums beat to battle, and he marched
  at my side.

German Soldiers' Song.

He came staggering blindly through the
village, past the dug-in anti-tank gun, his
face as if someone had thrown a handful of
red jam at it.

He was babbling incoherently to himself
and, although the gun-crew shouted at him,
he never deflected from his course. A
sergeant grabbed his arm, but he shook him
off. An officer bellowed an order at him, but
he did not seem to hear. He ran through the
village at his absurd, shambling jog-trot and
disappeared from sight. The officer and the
sergeant stood there in the middle of the
cobbled road and stared after him in puzzled
silence.

Five minutes later another two soldiers
appeared, running. One was without a helmet and both were without weapons. Their

grey trousers were wet up to the knees as if they had been wading through water. The officer rapped out a question at them and they mumbled something breathlessly, the sweat gleaming on the back of their necks. Then they, too, disappeared up the road.

'Them last two were stubble-hoppers – infantry,' one of the gun-crew whispered to his neighbour. 'They're doing a bunk up in the line, I betcha!' His neighbour did not say anything, but he looked anxiously up the road.

More and more came down the road into the village. Some ran, without helmets or weapons, frankly afraid. Others half-ran, half-walked, conscious of the eyes of the gunners upon them. Some were wounded, but they limped on, their eyes fixed on the ground as if they were ashamed of being wounded. The silent urgency of the men unsettled the gunners. One by one they clambered out of their trench and stood at the side of the road, asking questions in hushed timid voices like children in church. But not one of the retreating men answered their questions; it was as if they were afraid of being singled out and losing the anonymity of the crowd.

The officer and the sergeant stood in the centre of the road and tried to stop the fleeing soldiers, but they were buffeted and gradually forced to one side. One after another the gun-crew slipped into the crowd, tearing off their equipment as they went, until only the officer and the sergeant were left.

Then they saw an engineer colonel forcing his way ruthlessly through the jam in a captured jeep. The officer looked at the sergeant for a brief second and then they, too, joined the fleeing soldiers.

CLAUSEN

Leutnant Clausen stood there on the parapet of the trench, the machine-pistol held limply in his hand with blue smoke still curling softly out of the muzzle. His body trembled with the exertion and the excitement of the last ten minutes and he tried to get a grip on himself. With a practised flick of his forefinger and thumb he jerked his tight helmet back on his forehead, and looked in the direction from which the attack had come some ten minutes before.

Ten minutes ago, he thought. It seemed like ten years! Out of the early morning mist they had come with their long old-fashioned rifles and cumbersome ankle-length grey coats, and then all hell had been let loose. And now? He looked at the figures of the dead lying in the still misty undergrowth out in front of him, and then at the bloodied corpses lying tumbled in the trench behind him: Schulze, the cocky Berliner, Kroeger, the ex-sailor from Bremen, whom he had suspected of being a Red, and great big lumbering Heidemann, his sergeant. Just a mass of awkward limbs now.

Clausen breathed in deeply and felt the fresh morning air bite into his lungs, which were still full of the acrid cordite smoke of battle. He looked at his wristwatch. Zero seven hours. Seven o'clock on a spring morning somewhere in Germany. An April morning with the familiar red and white houses in the distance and the typical, dark fir wood on the left. Somehow it did not seem possible to him that anyone could die violently here among the so familiar surroundings, but a little voice inside him told him they could. Better get on your way, he told himself, before Ivan starts up again. He looked again at the scene around him and felt suddenly that this would be the last time for him. Clausen clipped a new magazine into his machine-pistol and slung it over his shoulder. Then he set off down the road that they had marched up the night before – nearly a hundred of them.

As he came to the bend in the road something prompted him to look back. He did so and saw a thin black dog silhouetted against the sky-line nuzzling one of the dead bodies. Something about it frightened him; it was like something from a medieval print. 'Get away!' he shouted. 'Go on!' But the animal just looked at him mutely. Losing patience he lifted his machine-pistol and fired a short burst in the animal's direction. The shots did not seem to scare the dog, but after a moment it loped away into the bushes. The beasts around here must be getting used to gunfire, he told himself as he went on his way. He felt better now. The doggerel the front-swine recited came to his mind. How did it go now?

'Watch in the chamber-pot – all money gone – mud under me hob-nails – deep in the heart gonorrhoea fear – good morning, good morning!'

It did not make sense, he knew, but it summed up for him the whole damn mess.

It was about two hours later that he was stopped at a road-block by a patrol of the Field Gendarmerie: big fellows all over one metre eighty, with silver plates on little chains round their necks. He was parched and asked for a drink, but they said he would have to answer a few questions first. Their tough manner did not scare him. It was funny really, he thought. At the front you always seemed to be finding yourself next to some chap with one leg or angina pectoris and yet at home you found the place full of these types.

They took him in front of a fat major, wearing a pince-nez, who did not offer him a seat and kept him standing to attention like the rawest recruit.

The major spoke softly, his head bent over the papers on his desk. 'You say your company was wiped out and … er … that you were the only one to survive.'

'Yes,' Clausen said laconically, somewhat amused at the major's tone which reminded him forcefully of his last teacher in the Gymnasium.

'Doesn't it,' the major began, pursing his lips as if he were thinking hard. 'Doesn't it seem rather strange, leutnant, that you were the only one to survive – especially as an officer? I'm sure you are familiar with the casualty rate among infantry officers?'

Clausen saw from the look on the man's face as he bent over the desk, and that of the captain standing next to him, that this was serious. They were not just asking him a few questions – they were trying him! They were after his head! His tiredness and cynicism left him in a flash.

'But it's true all the same, sir,' he said quickly. 'Of course some of the company might have got away. You see … we lost contact twice during the night when my position was overrun…'

The major smiled softly and looked at the captain knowingly. The captain returned his smile grimly, his hard face breaking into a series of deep cracks.

'Ah,' the major said like a headmaster

talking to a small boy. 'Now we are changing our story slightly, aren't we?' He paused for a moment and then continued in the same quiet tone as before. 'But no matter. Let me have your papers, please.'

Automatically Clausen's hand went up to his tunic pocket, and then he remembered.

'I'm afraid I can't ... let you have my papers, sir,' he stuttered. 'They were with the rest of my personal kit in my pack ... and they went with the rest, last night...' Lamely, he stopped speaking.

For the first time the major looked Clausen full in the face, and it was a face that he had seen often enough before in the last four years of war. It was a staff face, full of the letter of the law and the oath of loyalty to the Führer. He had seen the face everywhere in the officers' casinos and brothels from Omsk to Amiens. His heart sank.

'So they went with the rest that night,' the major echoed ironically. He was enjoying this. 'And that's where you left your trousers too, I suppose.' He looked down at the filthy grey trousers Clausen was wearing. 'You realize, don't you, that you are wearing the trousers of a common soldier although you are supposed to be an officer...?' He stopped suddenly as if he had discovered some heinous crime. 'Perhaps you're not an officer after all?' His voice took on a cunning note that people who suspect cunning in other

15

people often adopt. 'You are wearing the Knight's Cross with Oak Leaves. You possess the Iron Cross, Class One and Two – and yet you can't be more than twenty-two! Perhaps you...' His voice was like a sharp knife cutting delicately into some fine meat ... 'took the tunic of some dead officer and...'

Vehemently Clausen began to protest and then stopped short when he saw the look in the eyes of the two men facing him.

'I'll tell you what you are!' the major bellowed suddenly, his face going scarlet. 'You are a swine of a deserter – whether officer or not! No troop – no papers – no alibi!'

'Sergeant!' the thin captain snapped.

'Zu Befehl, Herr Hauptmann!' A tall M.P. sprang forward and stood there waiting for further orders.

The major scribbled briefly in the book in front of him, then raised his head and spoke:

'Prisoner Clausen, you are found guilty of treason. You are a traitor and a danger to the German Nation and our Leader, Adolf Hitler! You will be shot!'

Clausen gasped for breath. It could not be happening to him, he told himself wildly. It must be somebody else. He began to stutter meaningless words, and then moved forward to speak with the major. The sergeant misconstrued his motive and grasped him savagely by the arm, twisting it mercilessly behind his back. Clausen could not help it. He screamed. They led him away.

The major's lip curled into a sneer of disgust.

'My God, what a coward,' he said. 'And Adolf Hitler has to lead such a rabble to victory.'

Friedrich Clausen. Born 1922. Home town Schwarzenbek, near Hamburg. Eight years Grammar School. Abitur at 17. Intended to become a Marine Engineer. Instead Leutnant of Infantry. A front-swine of three Russian winters and a stomach and chest wound. Not much to put in an Obituary Notice, you might say.

April 24th, 1945.
The High Command of the Wehrmacht announces:

'...In the Mecklenburg area the 5th Red Guard Tank Army renewed its attacks and our forces in the region of Templin and Anklam were compelled to make strategic withdrawals.'

They got them off the train; every soldier irrespective of his rank – the S.S. did not bother about such things – and lined them up on the platform.

'Unit? Papers? Where are you going?' they asked.

'Compassionate leave! Ha, ha! That's a

good one. Right. Outside and get into the truck.'

'Next!'

'Vehicle Mechanics' Course! That's a nice little dodge, eh? Thought you were going to live the war out. Right. Outside and get into the truck.'

'Next!'

'Wounded. Where?'

'In the left arm.'

'Are you right or left-handed?'

'Left-handed. Why?'

'Right. Outside and get into the truck.'

That afternoon they collected three hundred men together in various states of ill-health and despair and joined them together with the survivors of a 'stomach battalion' – a battalion composed solely of stomach cases raked out of the military hospitals. They called them, with unconscious irony, 'Storm Group' Jawitz after the name of their commander. Next day they went into action with one rifle between every two men. The afternoon of the same day they went into action again, and this time there were rifles enough to go round and some to spare. The only men out of that Group who lived to see the end of April were those who surrendered to the Russians. They took their beating from the lousy cursing Russians without a murmur. It's worth it, they told themselves afterwards.

WOLF-BODO

It was Wolf-Bodo's idea, not ours. We sat on the hill-top and watched the Hungarians leave the bunker, throwing their equipment and rifles away as they went.

'Just like them,' Wolf-Bodo said and sneered. 'I often wonder why the Führer took up with such people.'

Wolf-Bodo was tall for sixteen, had blue eyes and wore his blond hair in a quiff swept over his brow like the Führer. 'Look,' he said after a moment's silence, 'what about us taking over the pill-box? We could do it easily – there are seven of us.'

I was a bit scared, but all the rest seemed enthusiastic, so I had to tag along.

'I'll tell you what we'll do – we'll go home, get some food and put on our uniforms. Then all back in an hour's time. All right?'

Everybody agreed and we went back to the village at the double.

It was like the times we went on picnics when we were kids. Everybody turned up in their Hitler Youth uniforms, sandwiches under arm and as excited as anything. Dierkin had brought a spear – he was always a bit too much interested in that cowboy and Indian stuff – and we all started laughing.

'What you got there?' Wolf-Bodo asked.

'I brought it … just in case,' Dierkin said

reluctantly. 'My granddad brought it back from Africa.'

The look on his face as he said this made us all laugh, and Wolf-Bodo said:

'Don't bother about weapons. I've been in the bunker and there are five "bangers" there.' He emphasized the word "banger", proud of knowing the soldier's word for rifle. 'Apart from them there's a Panzer-Fist, too.'

'Oh,' everybody said excitedly. 'Show us it.'

Wolf-Bodo crawled into the narrow entrance of the bunker on his hands and knees and reappeared a moment later with the weapon in his hand. He showed us how to put the bomb in and how to fire it.

'Whoever fires it,' he said, and we all knew that he would because he was the leader, 'must let the tank get pretty close otherwise it won't work. Just won't penetrate the armour.'

'Right,' he said, handing the Panzer-Fist to me, 'let's get ourselves sorted out. You,' he pointed to Dierkin and another boy, 'go and drag bushes across the road down there.' He indicated the spot with his forefinger.

'What for?' Dierkin asked.

Wolf-Bodo obviously did not mind answering the question. Probably he was flattered by the opportunity to show his knowledge.

'Well, you see when the tank sees the way

20

is blocked it will slow down, and that's our chance to do our job. Simple, eh?' Everybody was suitably impressed.

'Now don't forget,' he said in his leader's tone, 'plenty of bushes.' He turned to the rest of us. 'Right, we'll arrange guard duties now.'

I don't like confined spaces and the inside of the bunker smelt, so I slept outside. Nothing happened during the night except that Dierkin felt sick and fell asleep on guard.

Next morning we sat around miserably, eating our dry sandwiches, whilst Dierkin did an extra guard for his negligence of the night before. Suddenly he came running up with this stupid spear in his hand.

'Hey,' he shouted, 'there's a tank ... a tank!'

I was scared and felt like urinating, but Wolf-Bodo was on his feet at once.

'Where?' he asked, raising the yellow, mother-of-pearl opera glasses that he wore round his neck, like the officers in the pictures, to his eyes.

'Down there – about two hundred metres away!'

Wolf-Bodo focused his glasses and peered down the road for a minute.

'It's a Sherman,' he said. 'I recognize it from the wall-charts in the club-room.'

Everybody looked frightened.

'Right,' Wolf-Bodo snapped, 'everybody into the bunker.'

We all ran to it and crawled into the narrow entrance.

The tank stopped near the pile of bushes and then Wolf-Bodo fired. The blast from the Panzer-Fist hit me squarely in the face and I couldn't see for a minute. Then Wolf-Bodo and Dierkin were shouting wildly: 'We've got him! We've got him!' I pressed forward with the others to get a look out of the narrow slit. The tank was burning fiercely, and even at that distance we could hear the crackling as the tongues of flame licked the air. The ammunition started to explode and a mushroom of dense black smoke rose slowly into the air. I felt sick when I thought of what had happened to the men inside, but I pulled myself together.

'What are we going to do now?' I asked.

Wolf-Bodo laughed.

'What do you think? We're going to stay here and wait for the next tank to come along.'

'But,' I began to protest, but the rest cut me short.

'Yes,' they shouted, 'that's right, Wolf-Bodo. We're going to stay here and wait for the next tank to come along. And then knall! – another Ami gone.'

But there were no more tanks. About half an hour later we saw a line of khaki-clad figures advancing cautiously up the hill. As they came nearer we saw that dotted regularly along the line were soldiers with a kind of round pack on their backs and a hose in their hands.

'What's that?' Dierkin asked curiously and pointed.

Wolf-Bodo focused his glasses importantly, and then he went pale.

'What is it?' we asked.

'Flame-throwers,' he answered weakly.

Everybody paled. We all knew about flame-throwers. There was a fellow in the village who had had his face burnt in the First World War by one of those. We were all scared of him and did not like to go past his house at night.

'What are we going to do?' everybody asked. Dierkin began to cry – he was only fourteen.

Wolf-Bodo gulped and then seized a rifle.

'I'll tell you what we're going to do,' he said hoarsely, and I knew he was frightened too. 'I'll tell you what we're going to do,' and he rushed outside.

We crowded round the slit to see what he was going to do.

He knelt in the middle of the field and took aim. He fired and missed. And then again. This time one of the khaki-clad figures stumbled and fell. Wolf-Bodo turned his head to the bunker to say something and then it caught him. A great tongue of red and blue flame from the side licked at him and then wreathed him roundabout. It seemed ages before he screamed. It was terrible and I fainted.

The tiny eyes of the captain quartermaster set in the fat coarse face followed every movement of the boy as he went around the room, laying the table: the silver spoons 'liberated' aeons ago in France in 1940, the damask tablecloth 'borrowed' from the Polish countess who had been his mistress for many months in Warsaw, the heavy gold candlesticks 'organized' from a Russian museum in the campaign of 1941.

The boy moves like a damn woman, he thought. He felt dislike and yet attraction for him. The boy finished setting the table and stood to attention, waiting to be dismissed. The quartermaster lifted his gleaming booted foot heavily on to the footstool, and pointed with a fat forefinger in its direction. The boy sprang forward at once, turned about and took the boot between his legs. The quartermaster could feel the pressure of the boy's knees on his leg. Slowly, savouring the feeling, he put his other foot against the taut material across the boy's backside and pushed. The boot came off after a moments pressure. Quietly the boy set it down on the floor and took up his position again, with his legs astride.

The quartermaster let him wait for a minute, and then carefully slid his finely polished leg between the boy's knees. The boy took the strain, expecting the officer's other foot against his backside.

The quartermaster spoke:

'Will you?' he asked laconically.

The boy went rigid and then spoke without lifting his head up.

'Will I do what, sir?'

The quartermaster was irritated slightly at the boy's tone, but he did not really care either way.

'You know damn well what I mean,' he said. 'Everybody in the unit knows. Will you or won't you?'

The boy did not answer, but the officer sensed he knew. He raised his stockinged foot and placed it against the boy's backside. He did so gently and could feel the soft flesh through the material of the sock. He was about to press hard when the door was flung open suddenly. An excited sergeant stood framed in the doorway, his face flushed red.

'Sir,' he gulped. 'We've caught a couple of Polacks ... trying to loot the stores. Caught 'em red-handed with their mouths full of liver-sausage and their pockets full of cigarettes.'

The man's excitement irritated the quartermaster. Since he spent those months in Warsaw mixing with the Polish nobility, as he called his acquaintances to himself, he had hated any form of loudness.

'Shoot them,' he said briefly, and was about to dismiss the man with a wave of his hand when he had an idea.

'I think we'll let one or two of the younger members of the unit do the job this time, Sergeant. It's about time that some of them underwent their baptism of blood, eh?' He looked up cunningly at the face of the boy standing stiffly to attention near the footstool. 'Well, Moeller, would you like the job?'

The boy went pale and his eyes looked at the officer wildly.

'Yes,' the quartermaster said, drawing out the word. 'I can see you're eager. It would be something to write home and tell Mutti about, wouldn't it?'

There was a moment's silence.

'That's the way, Moeller,' the officer said god-humouredly. 'You're learning. A good soldier in the German army doesn't say thank you for a favour, he just comes smartly to attention and clicks his heels.' His voice suddenly became almost menacing. 'Doesn't he, Moeller?'

As if coming out of a daze the boy sprang to attention, bringing his heels together with a loud snap. The officer smiled at him and then seemed to lose interest. He waved a languid hand indicating dismissal. Briskly the sergeant and Moeller moved to the door. Then suddenly, as if he had just remembered something, the sergeant turned and spoke:

'Oh, by the way, sir,' he said. 'A mangy black hound got into camp somehow, sir, and is wandering around all over the show. What shall I do about it?'

'Hm,' the officer said, and thought for a moment. He shrugged his shoulders. 'Oh, while Moeller's about it he might as well do the dog, too.'

'Sir!' the sergeant said smartly, and then they went out.

The officer sat there contemplating his still booted foot on the footstool, and did not move until he heard two single rifle shots. He smiled and helped himself to a grape. Mustn't have got the dog, he thought.

Two days later the stores, Moeller and the quartermaster were blown to smithereens in a low-level attack by fighter-bombers.

The elderly stretcher-bearers brought them in from the train and laid them down in the large bare room which had once been the assembly-hall of the local Volksschule: row after row of them in their filthy, bloodied uniforms straight from the front. The waiting nurses started working their way down the rows, ripping and tearing every stitch off the wounded men. As they pulled the bandages away the men screamed shrilly like women and the nurses could see the lice running across the wounds.

There they lay, a hundred and sixty wounded men packed into that bare hall – white, bloodied bodies with that patch of black on the stomach which was so uniform and yet so individual – and waited. Then it came. The showers concealed in the roof began to flow and the men started to scream again as the cold water hit them squarely on the body. Some did not scream for long – they died. The nurses knew that some would die – they always did – but what could they do? There was no longer any time for individual treatment.

Meanwhile, the rest of the hospital sprang to life. The surgeons, who were to operate, and the nurses, who were to assist them, were wakened. They had a cup of coffee or a glass of cognac, as they fancied, and hurried downstairs. Underneath their white overalls they only had on their underclothes because of the heat that was generated by the lamps in the operating theatre.

And then it began: the shaving, the marking, the quick plunge into taut skin with the scalpel, the chopping, the gouging, the collapsing, the slicing. There was no time for the delicate, complicated surgery they had learnt so long ago in the Schools at Vienna, Cologne and Jena. It was the quick decision and then amputate. Hour in, hour out, the eight surgeons worked almost shoulder to shoulder under the glaring light in the tiny room until the sweat dripped into their eyes and they had to stop whilst the sister wiped their brows with a piece of lint.

At this time the boiler-man was busy, too, in his own peculiar fashion. He had been the school-caretaker and the hospital had taken him over with the rest of the school. Every hour or so the male orderly, with the steel-rimmed spectacles and stoop, would come down from the operating theatre and put the white-enamelled bucket carefully down on the floor. The boiler-man would laugh at the orderly's white sickly face and say: 'More for up the chimney, eh?' And he would circle his forefinger upwards in a spiral fashion like smoke going up a chimney. The orderly would leave without saying a word, and the boiler-man would laugh and repeat his phrase: 'More for up the chimney.' It was an old joke with him.

Taking a deep breath, he would open the boiler door and let the hot flames lick out for a moment or two. Then he would fling the contents of the bucket into the centre of the fire. Occasionally a piece stuck on the side of the bucket and he would have to scrape it out with his dirty hands. He did not mind. He had a cushy job at the hospital. That day over twenty men went up the chimney.

They said they would never forget.

'He saved us,' they said, as they dragged the dead man into the cover of the corn, and their eyes were full of tears of gratitude.

'If he hadn't gone out, they would have done for us – for sure,' they said and lit a stump of cigarette, shielding the flame with their cupped hands.

'Did you hear what he said before he ... went?' they said. 'He was a good comrade. I'll never forget him.'

But they forgot. They forgot the look in his eyes – the words he spoke – the way he died. They forgot.

Ein Volk auf der Flucht! A nation on the run! In the east and in the west they began to pour out of their villages and their cities; from their woods and their fields; from their factories and their streets. From East Prussia and Pomerania, from the Rhineland and the Ruhr, from Austria and Czechoslovakia, from Poland and the Baltic States. But where to go?

They wandered desperately between the fronts, sent scurrying in a different direction by each new change in the course of the battle. They would go south and someone would shout: 'The Ami's there already.'

They would move east again and hear: 'Ivan captured the village yesterday!' They would go north and be told: 'The Tommies are expected tomorrow!'

They ran and they died. They died in their thousands in the last seven days of that pleasant month of April. They were crucified as an example outside the bare wooden church on the hill, and the blood ran down their face from the nail hammered in the centre of their forehead. They were blown up, with the maddened horses, as they ran panic-stricken through the minefield. They were stealing turnips in the open fields when the machine-guns opened up and the stream of white tracer bullets brought them a quick death. They were raped by the side of the road and then slaughtered systematically. They were bombed, they were mined, they were burnt, they were bayoneted, they were machine-gunned, they were stabbed. They were killed by Russians, by Americans, by French, by British. They were killed by Germans. They ran and they died.

ILKA HARMANN
Softly Ilka opened the trap and crept downstairs. The door of her mother's bedroom was open and she could see the Russian, of the night before, flat out on his back, with Gerda and Leni snoring in his

31

outstretched arms. Even after the happenings of the night before she could still blush, and she lowered her eyes quickly as she passed the open door.

The body of the other Russian lay starkly in the kitchen, his head in a pool of blood. Suddenly she felt sick and rushed out into the fresh morning air.

The birds sang and in the distance a cock crowed, but as she walked along the path from the farm she was seemingly oblivious to them.

Then she saw Jussef. He came out of the bushes and grinned at her, which was strange in itself, for he had never done so before. She could only remember him with a scowl on his face when she and her mother had spoken to him. But today he was smiling. And why shouldn't he? Twelve hours a day on a starvation diet of soup and potatoes – and now he was free at last.

He waved his hand at her and said in his queer Polish-German:

'Fraulein, you come here.' Unsuspectingly she went to him.

'Yes, Jussef, what do you want?' she said, in the same mistress-servant tone she had used to him for the last five years. 'The Pole belongs to the Slavic Race and is consequently third-rate', they had learnt in the Middle School.

'Yes, Jussef,' she repeated somewhat

impatiently when he did not answer at once. And it was then that she saw the look in his eyes – a look that she had never noticed before in the five years that they had owned Jussef. She wanted to run, but all the strength seemed to have drained from her legs.

He had her on the ground and she began to fight desperately. She scratched and bit, and tried to jerk her knee up and catch him between the legs as her mother had always told her to do. But gradually he bore her down. Who would think that he still had so much strength after five years on black bread and potato soup?

She began to plead with him, forgetting that they had only taught Jussef the most necessary words in German and then laughed when he had mispronounced them.

'Jussef,' she gasped, her breath coming in great gulps. 'Let me go, please let me go … please… I'm a Catholic like you! What would Father Schmidt say…?'

But she forgot that Father Schmidt had once refused Jussef Confession and had kicked him out of the church after his – the Priest's – son had been killed on the Russian Front.

'Please,' she pleaded … 'please… Please… PLEASE!'

He started tearing wildly at her clothing.

She staggered down the main road among the crowd of refugees who flooded the roads everywhere. Her clothing was torn and her long hair hung down her back in wild disarray. She mumbled to herself and froth flecked her lips, but no one had time to bother about her. At every step she left behind her in the dust a little spot of bright red blood.

Ilka Harmann. Born 1927. Home town Dolle. Two years Middle School. Wanted to be a bride – a bride in white like in the illustrated papers. Instead raped one fine morning in April by a Pole named Jussef, who was shot four days later by the Russians for looting.

HAMBURG – SUNDAY

00.33 hours. Air Raid Warning. Full-scale attack with main targets Altona, Elmsbuettel, Town Centre and Harbour.

03.01 hrs. All Clear.

14.40 hrs. Air Raid Warning. Daylight attack by Flying Fortresses on the Harbour, Docks and Wharves. Factories in the Wilhelmsburg area bombed.

16.20 hrs. Air Raid Warning repeated.

17.22 hrs. All Clear.

18.38 hrs. General Air Raid Warning for the Hamburg district.

19.10 hrs. All Clear.

00.33 hrs. Air Raid Warning. Full-scale attack with main targets Altona, Elms-buettel, Town...

'It was still quiet. I was coming down the Heidenkampsweg when the searchlights went on over in the east and the flak started. I ran back to the bunker, got the doors closed and gave the order that nobody was to leave. As people started to get nervous because of the bombs dropping all around I pointed out how strongly the shelter was constructed.

'Everything outside started to burn. It was impossible to put the fires out because every minute more and more bombs were being dropped. From the neighbourhood people began pouring in. Some of them had already taken off most of their clothes because of the heat. They dragged one old woman out of the canal – she had been splashed with phosphorus – but she began to burn again as soon as she came out of the water so they had to put her back in again and leave her.

'The light went out and hot water began to trickle into the shelter through cracks in the brickwork. One or two women screamed, but I told them it was water from the fire hoses they were using outside to put the fires out. I don't think anybody believed me.

'I thought we possibly could break through the wall into the cellar next door and get out that way. I knocked a hole in it, but the cellar next door was already full of flames. The sight of the flames set the kids off crying, so I covered the hole up with an old tablecloth somebody gave me. It grew hotter and hotter and everybody was complaining of a terrible thirst. We tried to drink the water that was coming through the cracks in the wall, but it was too hot for most of us, and then somebody discovered what was floating in it – so nobody could drink it then.

'That was when they started to die. Some just went under the water without a murmur, but others started to scream and struggle with those around them. A soldier began shooting off his pistol in the dark and we had to hold him under the water until he drowned. Then the wall fell in and the flames licked against us – something like the roaring sound at the smithy…'

'No, that's about all. I don't remember much more until that fellow from Major Gruen's L.S. Regiment got me out.'

'Well, I don't know really. I suppose these days it's sometimes better if you can't see…'

The reporter got to his feet and nodded to the nurse. She got up off her box and, looking knowingly at the reporter, she grasped the man's hand. The blind man let himself be led away obediently.

The reporter watched the nurse's legs in

the short skirt as she walked up the slight incline, leading the blind man. Not a bad pair of legs, he thought, and then started wondering how he would do the article. That bit about the people panicking was out for a start and then...

Hundreds of dead lay on the streets of Hammerbruch that morning. They borrowed a heavy bulldozer from the Navy Yard at Wedel-Schulau and dug a mass grave there. As in the time of the Plague in the Middle Ages they burnt twigs of the juniper tree whilst they carried out this work.

They threw away their stick grenades. They threw away their 'banger', as they called their 08. rifle. They ripped off the proud bands on their sleeves, that they had worn in their campaigns all over Europe: 'Das Reich Division', 'Hitlerjugend', 'Grossdeutschland'. Secretly they tried to cut off the blood group tattoo on their upper arms which marked them as a member of the S.S. They climbed out of their tanks for the last time and clambered down the turret carefully, holding their arms on the back of their neck under the watchful eye of the man with the machine-gun. They fired the last shell out of the 88 and then broke the firing-pin. They levered the chronometer out of the control panel of the fighter plane and then blew the old 'box' up. The boy who had wanted to get the Iron Cross before he went back to school in 1940 and had done so at the cost of half his face, sold it to a British soldier for two cigarettes and thought he was making a good deal. The officer with the Knight's Cross and the Pour le Merite threw them, together with his epaulettes, into a ditch when the Mongolian guard was not looking. He was going to be careful now, he told himself. Ivan did not like officers. He was going to be careful – he was going to survive.

THE GENERAL
He wanted the rain to stop and he was 'goddam gonna see that it did stop'. He wanted to be the first to link up with the 'Commies' and here the rain was paralysing his tanks and heavy transport. Why, it might mean the difference for him of ending the war a three- or four-star general. He was a general the like of which we had never seen before. He wore a bright coloured helmet which he had designed himself – probably after reading too many Scientific Fiction stories. At his hips he had a couple of tarty pearl-handled revolvers – yes, that's it, like in the cowboy films – and then he wore a pair of light coloured riding breeches which were certainly not regulation issue. And he wanted the rain to stop. So he went to see the chaplain.

GENERAL: Look here, Father. I want the rain to stop.

CHAPLAIN: (with a weak smile). The Lord has his ways and means, sir, but I don't think...

GENERAL: (red in the face) Who the hell do you work for anyway? Are you an officer of the — army, or aren't you?

The next day a Divisional Prayer appeared:

'Almighty and most merciful Father, we humbly beseech Thee, of thy great goodness, to restrain these immoderate rains with which we have to contend. Grant fair weather for battle. Graciously hearken to us as soldiers who call upon Thee that, armed with Thy power, we may advance from victory to victory and crush the oppression and wickedness of our enemies and establish Thy justice among men and nations. Amen!'

It stopped raining. And that was about that.

JIMMIE

Jimmie stood next to Lieutenant Green at the cross-roads and gripped his rifle at the port across his chest. They could hear singing now in the distance and then the columns came in sight, marching down the three roads that centred on the crossroads.

As they came nearer, Lieutenant Green turned to the Dutch sergeant-interpreter and asked:

'What are they singing, Klass?'

The sergeant cocked his head on one side and listened for a minute.

'Oh, one of those Nazi songs, sir,' he said. 'Something about marching off somewhere and the girls waving goodbye and all that guff.' The interpreter's too-perfect English accent irritated Green somewhat and he turned away without saying thanks.

They were quite close now and one or two soldiers were running up the road towards them, without weapons, shouting:

'Tick-tock for Tommie. You got tick-tick for Tommie?'

Green went red.

'You men,' he bellowed at the top of his voice. 'Come back here at once and stop that!'

The men stopped running and looked back over their shoulders. When they saw that it was Green who had shouted, they turned round and started to walk back down the road slowly and reluctantly. Jimmie grinned to himself.

'No loot for them today,' he said half-aloud.

'What's that you say?' Green asked.

'Nothing, sir,' Jimmie said. 'I was thinking aloud.'

'Hm,' Green said, and then turned to look up the road again. God, what a rabble to have to lead, he told himself.

The first German column began to march past. First came the officers – mostly tall and elegant in their riding breeches and polished jackboots and their yellow collar patches gleaming brightly in the sun. Their chests were festooned with medals and decorations: sports medals, wound medals – black for one wound, silver for three, gold for six – Russian Campaign medals, Close Combat Bar, and all kinds and degrees of crosses. As they marched they swung their arms rigidly across their bodies. Then, after the officers, came row after row of the rank and file in tattered grey uniforms, mostly boys of sixteen and seventeen and men of forty and fifty. Most of them did not even wear the regulation jackboot, but an ordinary leather boot with a kind of cloth gaiter attached. Every one of them had a grey loaf of bread sticking out of the cloth bag at his side.

Interspersed among the column were trucks and carts pulled by lean horses, with a pile of straw in the back upon which lay the sick and wounded and an occasional woman soldier.

The contrast between the appearance of the officers and the rank and file was so striking that Jimmie could not help saying to Green:

'What a difference there is, sir, between the officers and the ordinary soldier. You wouldn't have thought that the ordinary bloke would have fought so hard.'

Green turned.

'Perhaps they fought better because of the difference.'

Suddenly there was a crackle of gunfire up the road. A man in the grey of the German Army was running wildly down the road, past the column, with a pistol in his hand. Jimmie slipped of his safety-catch and raised his rifle to his shoulder. Green tugged at his thirty-eight. But he could not get it out.

'Fire – damn you!' he shouted at Jimmie. 'Go on, for Christ's sake!'

Reluctantly, Jimmie sighted. He knew he could not hit the running man's legs and he aimed at the chest. He squeezed the trigger and the man dropped in the dust and lay still. He lowered the rifle and looked at Green. He was sweating. The last time, he told himself. The last time for me.

THE BLIND MAN

'Take me with you, comrade!' the blind man pleaded.

He stood there at the side of the road, with his face black-pitted from the mine that had exploded in it the year before, and listened to the sound of the passing feet. Shuffling, dragging feet sending up little clouds of dust

42

as they staggered along.

He tried to visualize the scene, but he could not. He craned an ear to one side as if hearing better might help him to see the scene in his mind's eye. It did not.

He decided to try again.

'Take me with you, comrade! Please!'

This time someone answered him. It was an old man's voice.

'You can't come with us, boy,' it said. 'You can't come with us...' It trailed away.

'Take me with you,' the blind man pleaded again.

But nobody answered. Somewhere a soldier began to sing in a high-pitched hysterical voice.

'In der Heimat gibt's ein Wiedersehn.'

But he sang alone uncannily in the silence of the hundreds of shuffling feet.

Once the blind man was spoken to in a foreign tongue, but he did not understand what was said to him. It must be one of the foreign soldiers, he thought.

He transferred his bundle to the other shoulder and tried again. He waited for a moment and then spoke:

'Take me with you, comrade!'

'It's no use, lad. We can't take you with us. We're going...' the voice seemed to have difficulty finishing the sentence ... 'we're going from Germany.' The voice trailed away in the distance. 'We're leaving Germany...'

43

All that day he stood there in the hot sun, asking his question as the prisoners passed him in long columns. A man fell out dead near his feet, but he did not seem to notice. Somebody thrust a crust of bread into his hand, but he dropped it a moment later into the dust.

Mechanically, he repeated his question over and over again, no longer waiting for a reply, and the tears coursed down unseen from his blind eyes.

'Take me with you, comrade!'

'Wars are finally decided by one side or the other recognizing that they cannot be won. We must allow no moment to pass without showing the enemy that whatever he does he can never reckon on capitulation. Never! Never!

Adolf Hitler. Dec. 12th, 1944

CHAPTER II

MAY

We're gonna get lit up when the lights go
on in London.
           English Popular Song, 1945.

The War is over! Der Krieg ist aus! La
Guerre est...
    That night they celebrated: Ivan in Berlin,
Tommy in Hamburg and the Ami in Mun-
ich. And didn't they get drunk that night!
    Everywhere there was noise, although it
was three o'clock in the morning. The night
sky was lit up with white tracer bullets and
red and green Very flares. At every street
corner somebody seemed to be firing a sten-
gun in the air.
    The adjutant came to a semblance of at-
tention in front of the colonel. He was
stupid drunk, but the colonel did not appear
to notice or to care. He saluted vigorously
and nearly fell over with the effort he put
behind it.
    'Sir, I have to report that we already have
... er ... thirteen men in the guard-room for
drunk and ... disorderly conduct and ... B

Company have just started mortaring C Company and er...' The adjutant grinned foolishly – he had forgotten the rest of his report.

The colonel did not say anything. He seemed to be listening to something. Suddenly he put his forefinger up to his lips in mock conspiratorial fashion.

'Sh!' he said, and jerked his thumb in the direction of the window.

Outside they could hear the drunken singing of soldiers. The colonel made out the words, and then he started singing. After a moment's hesitation, the adjutant joined in.

Oh, when this bloody war is over.
Oh, how happy we will be...
We will tell the sergeant-major...
Oh, how happy we will be.

And they – 'they', the Jerries, Squareheads, Krauts, Heinies, Boches, Huns, Goons, as they were called at various time – what of them?

Well, they just wanted to survive now. The ones who wanted to die had done so in the first few days of May. The burgomaster committed suicide in his office after slitting the throat of his wife and daughter. The camp commandant had his last party and died with his painted young men all around him. The judge flung himself through the window as they came to fetch him; he had made his last decision. The quartermaster died defending his food store against the ragged survivors of a Panzer Grenadier Regiment who wanted food at all costs. He died fulfilling Paragraph D of Divisional Order Ten: 'Destruction of Food Dumps in the Face of the Enemy.' Grossbauer Schaumann was beaten to death by two Poles in his own farmyard whilst his own farmworkers looked on.

'Help me! Help me!' he screamed in his pain, but nobody did so.

As he was dying they mutilated him with a razorblade: 'Made in Germany. A Product of Solingen.' The women flung their aprons in their faces and dared not look, and then, when the screaming had stopped, they, too, started to loot.

At the conclusion of the singing, General Jodl stood to attention, addressed General Smith, and said in English:

'I want to say a word.'

He then lapsed into German, later translated as:

'General! With this signature the German People and German Armed Forces are for better or worse delivered into the Victor's hands. In this war, which has lasted five years, both have achieved and suffered more than perhaps any other people in the world. In this hour I can only express the hope that the Victor will treat them with generosity.'

THE SERGEANT

The sergeant watched them from one corner of the parade-ground. They had stopped shouting, now that Hermann was finally dead, and moved slowly and menacingly towards the commandant's office. As they walked they seemed to crouch like a boxer at the beginning of a fight when he sizes up his opponent.

The alarm siren, which had been going the whole time, suddenly tailed away to nothing, and the Goon guards, lined up outside the commandant's office, seemed startled, like a man who finds that he is walking naked down the main street and can't do anything about it, as in a dream. One of them jerked his bolt nervously, and the officers turned round and whispered angrily to him.

The sergeant watched, with a look of distaste on his face, the growing nervousness of both sides as they got closer and closer together. The officer licked his lips and gave an order hoarsely. Jerkily the soldiers lifted their rifles to their shoulders. The officer took up the megaphone.

'Listen, boys,' he shouted, with only a faint

German accent.

The sergeant's face curled into a sneer. So it was 'boys' now, was it?

'Try to be reasonable. The war is virtually over, I know, but we must try to retain some discipline. It's for your own good. If I and my guards left you now, you would be very much at the mercy of the civilian population and the Poles who...'

But the shouts and jeers of the advancing men drowned the rest of his words.

'You getting scared, you Goon bastard, you?' they shouted. 'We're coming to get you, boy. It's your turn now!'

The officer gave the order to load in a shaky voice. The soldiers obeyed and looked scared. They pulled the bolts back noisily. For a moment the advancing men faltered, but then those at the back pushed and they came on again.

'Please, don't come any further – please! Or I'll have to give the order to fire!' the officer almost screamed at them.

'You daren't fire,' somebody from the back of the crowd shouted. 'It'd be the long jump for you mate!'

Then one of the old soldiers of the guard panicked and fired. A man in the front rank of the crowd clutched at his knee and then crumpled up slowly on to the ground. The officer turned, startled, and bellowed at the man who had fired, but his words were lost in the great roar that went up from the advancing men – like that of an hysterical crowd at a football match out for blood. They broke into a run.

One or two of the guards fired, but most of them were too paralysed to do anything except stand there stupidly with their rifles in their hands until the crowd engulfed them. The sergeant, standing there in the corner, saw one of the guards dash out from the centre of the mob: a fat, elderly man. His spectacles had been cracked and broken from a blow and he ran blindly with his hands outstretched like a man feeling his way in a dark room. He was almost across the square, and the sergeant thought he might make it to the safety of the huts. But no! He stumbled and fell heavily in the dirt. He lay there, seemingly winded, and then they were upon him, thrashing and beating the prostrate body with the broad wooden staves that they had ripped out of their beds. Five years of confined rage, pent-up energy, impotency and desire finding an outlet in the beating of this fat German. The guard bellowed and screamed high like a woman in pain, and then he was silent. Slowly the crowd of men around him broke up, cursing and breathing heavily, and drifted back to the commandant's office. The guard lay still on the ground – either dead or unconscious. For a moment the sergeant felt pity for the man, but the next instant he hated himself for doing so. The fat swine would have done the same if the position had been reversed, he told himself. They're all the same – sickeningly, disgustingly bad. So bad that it made him feel like spewing his guts whenever he thought about it.

He turned and looked at the scene around the commandant's office. A man lay stretched out in the dirt, a pool of blood haloing his head. He was probably dead from the way he lay. Otherwise the guards seemed to have escaped with a good beating. Now they were limping away, their uniforms torn and bloodied, their hands supporting battered faces.

A circle of laughing, cheering men had the commandant stripped in a corner – the sergeant noticed he had terribly thin, spindly legs for a man of his enormous bulk – and were painting the letters P.W. – prisoner of war – on his naked chest in black paint.

From inside the office came the sound of smashing wood and breaking glass. Through the door came flying the prisoners' files and other documents, photographs of Hitler and a Nazi flag, upon which men began to spit, forcing the trembling commandant to look on as they did so.

Then a roar went up from the crowd. From a smashed window a man started handing out bottles. They've found the camp's spirit store, the sergeant realized. The men bellowed and fought to get a bottle. Someone dropped and smashed a bottle on the concrete step. Two men began to fight over the possession of a bottle. A man knocked the neck off his bottle on a stone and took a long drink from the jagged opening, seeming not to care that his lips were cut and bleeding.

A prisoner staggered past the sergeant, a German steel helmet on his head, a bottle in his left hand, a box of cigars in the other, and gripped between his teeth an unlit cigar stump. He swayed as he stood there looking at the sergeant stupidly. He seemed drunk already, whether from the excitement or the booze, the sergeant did not know. With a grandiose gesture he offered the bottle to the sergeant. The sergeant shook his head. He offered the box of cigars. Again the sergeant refused.

With a forceful gesture of his mouth the man spat the unlit cigar stump into the dirt and said:

'What's the matter with you, Jack? You got the hump or something?'

The sergeant said nothing.

'Cheer up,' he said. He made a low animal sound. 'Be getting in bed with the missus this time next week – an' I won't bother takin' me shoes off first, I can tell you. Come on,' he bellowed. 'We're free! The war's bloody well over and we're free!' He laughed uproariously and then after a second he staggered off in the direction of the Russian women's compound.

The sergeant watched him go and then laughed cynically to himself.

'So this is freedom,' he said aloud to nobody in particular, and his eyes traced a circle round the camp: to Hermann, the Goon sergeant-major, hanging starkly from the watch-tower, whom it had taken them twenty minutes to garrotte; to the man on the ground with his long blond hair trailing in the blood; to the fat commandant standing naked and sweating to attention in the middle of the parade-ground, where they were forcing him to stand until he dropped; to the men themselves, shouting and screaming as they dressed themselves up in bits and pieces of German uniform and civilian dress which they had looted from the guards' quarters. So this was freedom. The Jerries had had their day, too. They had beaten, starved and tortured, and now it was our turn to do the same. That was freedom.

The night was loud with laughter, drunken songs and screams. Every once in a while someone would loose a volley of rifle shots into the air, and now the camp searchlights, which had played on their wooden huts every night for the last five years, danced drunkenly about the night sky. They had

broken into the Russian women's compound and now they were everywhere in the
camp, squirming and rolling on the floor
with the heavy, uncomprehending, foreign
women.

The sergeant came to his decision sitting
alone in the smelly latrine made from Red
Cross packing-cases – the only place where
he could be alone that night. He took his
bundle and placed the treasured civilian
peaked cap on his head, and walked out of
camp without even a second look behind
him. Above him as he went out of the gate
hung the body of Hermann swaying ever so
slightly in the night breeze. He did not even
notice the black hound that waited in the
shadows at the side of the gate until he
passed before padding into the camp.

In 1936, when he was eighteen, he had
joined the Guards. A group of lads from the
village had come up one Saturday morning
for the match, but it had been cancelled so
they went and spent the rest of their money
in the boozer. Somebody got the idea that
they should join the Guards – even Geordie,
who wasn't the size of twopenny-worth of
copper, went along. As it worked out, he was
the only one to be accepted. At that time
there weren't many lads in his village really
healthy; all the others were turned down on

medical grounds.

He liked the Guards from the very first day he went on the square. It seemed he was a born soldier and his N.C.O.s told him so. He never went through the awkward stage that most young soldiers go through in the first weeks. His uniform fitted him as if he had been poured into it. He never dropped his rifle when the R.S.M. shouted an order. He never complained when they had to polish the metal buttons on their under-shirts or scrub the floor of their hut out with toothbrushes as a punishment. The others used to make fun of him, but they were impressed all the same by the way he did things. He was not on the peg once in the training depot.

When he left Caterham for the battalion, he was promoted to corporal almost at once. This caused a minor sensation in the battalion, where it was customary to have to wait for years before one was promoted. Mostly you were lucky if you ended up lance-sergeant at the finish of your 'Twenty-One'. He loved the army – well, perhaps not the army – the Guards. Squad drill on a bright spring morning was for him what classical ballet is to a balletomane. The precision and subtlety of movement of the tall, lean men, their heads well back under the cheese-cutters, represented for him somehow an order and certainty about life that he had never known in the grimy mining village that had been his home in Yorkshire. It made him feel that this was how the world would be – clean and well-scrubbed, ordered and neat.

'You've found an 'ome in the army, Corp,' the other blokes in the barrack-rooms used to kid, and he would laugh and say:

'Like hell!'

But he knew he had. The army was his life. In 1939 the battalion went over to France and he was made sergeant. In 1941 they went out to Egypt and got their knees brown. Two years later they were in Italy.

In the winter of 1943 they were engaged in bitter fighting in the mountains with the remnants of a fanatical German Parachute Regiment. If you opened your mouth and breathed in the ice-cold air it threatened to tear the lungs out of you. Expose your body to the cold too long in the performance of your natural functions and you ended up in hospital, your bladder and stomach in-flamed and terribly painful.

But the little group of men in the home-made camouflage suits sprawled exhausted in the snow did not seem to feel the cold. They lay there, waiting, their shoulders, which were gouged by the straps of their packs, heaving with the effort of running.

The young officer stood on the slope, careless of snipers, and looked at them, waving his swagger-cane to and fro as if drawing designs in the air.

'Sergeant,' he drawled in the affected voice that the young Guardee acquires within two months of being posted to 'town'. 'Sergeant,' he repeated when the man did not move. His 'rs' threatened to become 'ws'.

Wearily the sergeant forced himself up from the snow and staggered over to the officer.

'Sir,' he said hoarsely, licking his lips, which were cracked and chapped.

The young Guardee paid no attention to the sergeant and turned to the elderly American major, who stood next to him in his bright fawn coat, which had caused a big laugh when the boys had first seen it.

'Well, sir,' he drawled, 'you can see the position. Jerrry holds the ridge' – he waved his stick languidly in that direction – 'and it's our job to winkle them out. He's quite well dug-in, of course, and he has a couple of automatics, too. Quite an interesting tactical problem, don't you think?'

The major nodded his head, obviously impressed by the young officer's manner.

The Guardee continued:

'We've had three bashes at them already' – he waved his stick in the direction of the corpses which littered the hillside – big, lanky Guardsmen's corpses. 'But I think we're wearing them down. My chaps are quite good, you know.'

The major nodded and said nothing, his eyes fixed on the men crouched in the snow like beaten animals.

'Right, Sergeant,' the young officer snapped, all affectation suddenly gone. 'Get the men on their feet.'

The sergeant's mouth flopped open stupidly, but he pulled himself together quickly.

'Permission to speak, sir,' he said quite smartly.

'Yes, Sergeant,' the officer said, somewhat irritated by the sergeant's manner.

'Well, sir,' he began rather slowly, and the officer waved an impatient hand to hurry him up. 'The platoon's about had it, sir. We're down to half-strength. Couldn't we get the Hurries, sir, to blow them out?'

The officer shook his head:

'Imposs. – the Div.'s got no authority for an air-strike.'

The sergeant spoke again.

'Permission to speak, sir.'

'Yes, yes!' the officer snapped, conscious of the American's eyes upon him. 'Get on with it man!'

'Well, sir, what about softening 'em up with gunfire and then going in under cover of smoke.'

The officer looked at the sergeant for a long moment, and then blurted out:

'Dammit, man, are yer windy?' The

58

officer's pale, handsome face flushed red. 'Well, are you?'

The sergeant retained his weary look, but inside his mind was racing wildly. Out of the corner of his eye he could see his platoon lying there patiently in the snow and beyond, the bodies of the men who had died the hour before. A good N.C.O. should always see to his men first, it said in the book which was his bible.

'Permission to speak, sir,' he said automatically, not waiting for the officer to answer. He knew he had to do it. 'I can't take my lads up that hill again, sir,' he said simply. And with that he walked away from the officer and sat down again with the men to wait.

They gave him nine years. It was the talk of the clubs from Cairo to Naples for almost a week.

'I say, old boy, did you hear?' – taking another sip of the whisky and soda. 'A sergeant in the Guards, too. Regular as well. What next, eh?'

'Oh, do have another whisky, old man. Tell that wog over there.'

They stripped him naked and made him double-mark time, with his hands held stretched out above his head, whilst they made a pretence of searching his clothes. They made him bend down with his legs wide astride, whiles a corporal searched his body. They said it was to see if he had any contraband tobacco, but it was really the start of the systematic attempt to break and brutalize the prisoner. They lined the prisoners up, facing the open pens of the latrine, and then doubled them off, six at a time, and there they carried out their natural functions whilst two dozen other men looked on from six feet away. At the end of their three minutes they were doubled back and another six took their place on the still warm seats. The mornings and afternoons they spent in stupid futile drill and marching under the glaring hot Italian sun.

'Salute to the right! Up – two – three – four – five! Down – two – three! Salute to the left! Up – two...'

After the bread and margarine tea they were each given a filthy rusty dixie or a great holed baccy tin and expected to hand them back – these useless objects fit only for the rubbish dump – sparkling and bright like new. During this time the 'Staffs' – all the camp personnel were called staff-sergeant whatever their rank – prowled up and down outside in gym shoes, peering through the Judas-hole every so often, trying to catch them not working.

Day in, day out. Month in, month out.

There were six of them in their cell in that jail outside Naples, and the cell was only meant for two. They were locked in at nine at night, with the sun still shining outside and the sound of the girls' wooden heels on the pavement, until half-past five in the morning, with only a stinking bucket for their sanitary needs. They took turns in carrying it out in the mornings – two at a time. If they spilt it in the stone corridor outside, the corporal in charge of opening-up would make them dry the mess up with their bare hands. The sergeant was not soft, but he was forced to vomit every time he had to do this.

After six months they gave him a cushy job in the stores. They even talked of making him a staff if he got a remission of sentence. After all, he had been a sergeant in the Guards, and he hadn't been crimed once in his stay in the camp. They often made former inmates guards when they were released. Usually they were the fly boys, who had somehow managed to square the guards whilst they had been inside. If they had ever given him the chance, he would have refused. He felt no desire to rehabilitate himself in the army.

In the months he had spent in the Glass-house, he had gradually come to the realization of something he had never known before. What he had admired before, he hated now. He felt that there had been some justice in the decision to sentence him to jail, but this...! Now, he realized that the prison, with its calculated brutality, was what made the Army function. This was what lay behind the fine red coats sparkling in the sun on the parade-ground. All their Trooping the Colour and all their 'Three cheers for the C.-in-C., His Majesty, hip, hip!' – all that depended on the outraged body, the stained hands... For him the army was life and when it crumbled, he crumbled too. His hatred spread and became a hatred of men generally. He hated them for what they did, what they said, what they were...

After he had served nine months they offered to release him on suspended sentence if he volunteered for a front-line unit. They often did this. He volunteered and deserted to the enemy the first time he went into action again.

FARMER GIER

Farmer Gier looked at the woman, standing before him bent and humble. He did not rise to his feet when she came in or try to speak High German to her, although he could see that she was not from thereabouts.

'Na,' he grunted. 'And what do you want, my fine lady?'

'Please could you sell me some milk?' the woman asked timidly and clutched nervously at the purse in her hand.

'Ha, ha!' he laughed heartily, though his eyes remained cold and calculating. 'That's a good one, that is. And where do you think I should find milk? Tell me that, eh?'

The woman paused for a moment and then spoke again, her voice calculated not to give offence.

'But I saw a couple of cows outside on the meadow. That's why I came here. They looked such fine animals,' she added as an afterthought, smiling vaguely and hoping that the compliment might work.

'Those things!' the farmer's face assumed a look of contempt. 'They haven't enough milk to suckle a sparrow. I bet you could do a better job yourself.'

He saw by the look on her face that she wasn't used to that sort of talk. Well, my fine Madam, he told himself, here's where you start learning.

'Please,' the woman said, and for a moment he thought she was actually going to go down on her knees. He would have liked that. 'Please find me some milk. A litre is all I need. I've been walking all day. It's my husband. He's...'

He could see from the hesitant way she spoke that she wasn't used to making personal confessions.

'He can't digest anything else ... since he was wounded in forty-three and the army doctor said…'

'What the devil do I care about your husband or his damned wound either! Your type and their Nazi friends started this thing, and I say let them suffer a bit for it now!'

Farmer Gier had been one of the clever ones. He managed to keep out of the Party, but still he had enjoyed all the benefits it had to offer: cheap labour, subsidies, exemption from the army. He thought for a moment that the woman was going to argue. He was amused to see how far he could go with her.

'I can pay for it,' she said hurriedly. 'I don't want anything for nothing. How much would a litre of milk cost? Tell me that, please?'

The farmer chuckled.

'Why, certainly. I can tell you that. Forty-five pfennigs. Exactly forty-five pfennigs, Reichs pfennigs a litre, Gracious Lady.'

The Gracious Lady was a little bit of irony on his part, but she did not seem to notice it. She searched in her purse and took out a coin. She held it out.

'Here,' she said. 'Here's a one mark piece. You can keep the change.'

Involuntarily she fell into the tone she had used with waiters and servants all her life. It annoyed him and he took the coin and flung it into the corner.

For a moment the woman seemed about

to say something, and then with a sigh she went and picked the coin up.

'How much do you want?' she asked in the same subdued tone as at first. 'Two – three – five marks?'

The farmer took his time. He cut himself a large slice from the white meat of the chicken that stood on the table in front of him to show her what kind of a man he was.

'How much yer got?' he asked with his mouth full.

The woman thought for a moment. He could see that she was considering whether she should tell the truth or not.

'About fifty-six marks and a few pfennigs,' she said.

He shook his head.

'Not enough,' he said. He enjoyed the look on her face.

'In heaven's name what do you want then?' she asked frantically. And then as if she had had a sudden idea, she began to unstrap the little gold watch on her wrist.

'What about this?' she said. 'It's real gold. I got it from … the day I was eighteen.'

His eyes glinted with greed, but he shook his head. Now he was after bigger things. He pretended to examine it and pursed his lips with pretended regret.

'Sorry,' he said, 'I'm afraid it's not enough.'

The tears started up in her eyes and her face seemed to crumple.

'What do you…?' but she was unable to go on.

'Do I want?' he completed the sentence for her brutally. 'I want you!'

'Me!' she said uncomprehending. 'Me!'

'Yes, you,' he said, rising from his chair. 'I want you with me in there' – he pointed to the open door which led to the bedroom with the great double bed– 'And consider yourself lucky that I've taken a fancy to you. Why, I can get a great big farm lass any night of the week for five cigarettes … with bubs that would make three of those skinny dugs of yours!'

Her brain raced wildly. She wanted to protest – to scream – to run, but then she saw in front of her the pale, sickly face of her husband lying inert in the corner of their one room. The army doctor had said he had only one or two months left.

She started to cry softly to herself, but she did not protest as he began to lead her into the next room.

Their whole life began to centre around food. They talked about it, read about it, thought about it, dreamed about it. And all the time there was that terrible gnawing monster in their bellies, who just could not be satisfied with artificial honey and boiled cabbage.

They began to steal. Every night they

would crawl into the fields and steal the turnips and new potatoes out of the earth, putting them into cloth bags that hung around their necks. It did not matter much if the farmer's dogs worried them – they had to have food.

They began to barter their possession for it. At first it was rather funny in its way to be standing at the street-corner selling odds and ends like a newspaper boy. But when everything started to go – even the furniture – it was no longer funny. It was said that the farmers now furnished their stables with Persian carpets because their houses were full, and that the cattle drank their water out of marble basins.

They began to sell themselves. That slim handsome boy over there, with the fingers of his right hand gone and the thin, supple cane – the mark of his profession – in his left. That blonde girl over there with the pigtails of a schoolgirl and ravaged eyes. That woman with the moth-eaten fur tippet for all the heat of the day – it is to hide the marks of the rope on her neck – and the pointed-toe, patent-leather shoes that were fashionable in the 'twenties. They must have food.

Simple arithmetic.

'Now pay attention, children!

'To live you have to buy on the Black Market. And on the Black Market a pound of butter costs 259 marks, a loaf of bread 60 marks, a pound of coffee 250 marks. The average working man, however, earns 50 marks a week. The problem is, children – how long would the average working man live?'

Simple arithmetic.

CLAUSEN

Clausen was free. The morning that they had been going to shoot him a British tank force had arrived and the whole lot of them – prisoner and guard alike – had been sent to a prison cage. The young British officer who had taken over the jail had been interested in Clausen's story and for some reason or other had arranged it that he should be released early.

And now he was on his way home with a loaf of stale white bread, a tin of corned beef in his knapsack and forty marks and a discharge certificate in his pocket.

He was free, and he simply could not believe it. Even the journey through the ravaged suburbs of Hamburg could not depress him. When he got home, he told himself, he'd put up his feet in the garden for a bit and then he'd look around for a job – but there was no hurry about that. Or perhaps he might be able to get a place in the University. Oh, well, plenty of time to think about that later.

He ate his loaf of bread in the crowded train to Schwarzenbek, with the people hanging on the buffers and clinging to the roof, but the tin of corned beef he decided to keep as a surprise for Mutti. But it was Clausen, not Mutti, who was surprised. His mother was dead; blown up with the house by a direct hit in the last days of April. They hadn't even been able to find the bits to bury her. But of course they didn't tell him that.

He was stunned. It was as if someone had beaten him for a long time over the head with a large stick. The neighbours were kind and offered to take him in, but he declined. He went straight back to Hamburg on the next train.

After a day or two he decided he could no longer just sit around brooding in the bunker. He must get a job – bury himself in work and forget. What could he do? he asked himself. Perhaps he could study. At the University they told him he could not. As a regular officer he was forbidden by the Military Government to study. He protested that he was only seventeen when he had joined the army and could not possibly have known his own mind. The clerk at the counter looked at him over his spectacles, shrugged his shoulders and turned his back on him.

Clausen was not discouraged. It had been

easier after the First World War when ex-officers had become gigolos and dance-partners: 'Kiss the hand, madame' and all that. But still, he told himself, if he couldn't work with his nut he would have a go working with his hands.

By a stroke of luck he got a job in a factory where they were converting steel helmets into saucepans. He was very happy that day, and passed the rest of the afternoon spending his remaining few marks on a plate of potato soup, which tasted like hot water, and a couple of glasses of beer, which tasted like cold water. He started making plans again. He would stop living in the bunker and get himself a little room somewhere or other. He'd keep his studies up the best he could and perhaps later when things were different – in five or six months' time – he could have another go at the Uni...

By the time the dinner-hour came along on that first morning he was exhausted from lifting the heavy crates up and down, but he was happy. He sat down with the other men behind the stack of crates and opened his little newspaper packet of sandwiches: three slices of dry bread and one with jam. He hate them hungrily, helping them down with mouthfuls of water from his water-bottle. He was just about to start on his jam sandwich, which he had saved to the last so as to have a pleasant taste in his mouth for the rest of the afternoon, when the runner from the office came up.

He jerked his thumb in the direction of the office and said:

'Wanted in the office.'

Clausen thanked him and put his sandwich away carefully. Wanted in the office, he repeated to himself as he walked up the yard. It was like the army all over again. Always the little man's fear that the organization was going to make some new demand upon him.

He knocked at the glazed door and went in. The man behind the desk smiled and said:

'Oh, yes. Mr Clausen, isn't it?'

He returned the smile. It isn't like the army after all, he told himself. Even called me Mr.

'Sorry to trouble you in the dinner-hour,' the clerk said, 'but you know how it is.'

Clausen did not, but he mumbled something.

'Ever since the big raids started,' the clerk went on, 'my memory seems to be getting worse and worse. The attacks must have had some effect on me mentally. Seem to forget everything. The bombing was hell, you know.'

'Yes, the bombing was the worst,' Clausen agreed earnestly, in no way cynical.

'Well, to come to the point. I forgot to ask

71

you about your Hamburg residence permit before you started here. I wonder if I could just make a note of the number now?' He laughed. 'You won't give me away to the boss, will you?' he joked.

Clausen frowned.

'Hm,' he said, biting his lip. 'I'm afraid I haven't got one. You see I didn't have the time,' he went on hurriedly. 'I got the job and...'

He could see that the other man was not listening to him any more and he stopped speaking. It seemed ages before the clerk spoke again.

'I tell you what,' he said cheerily. 'You go up to the permit place this afternoon and I'll see if I can keep your job open for you... The boss is a bit of a stinker...'

'What do you mean?' Clausen asked puzzled. 'You'll keep my job open for me. Am I sacked or something?'

The other man nodded.

'I'm afraid you are,' he said slowly. 'You see, we can't employ anybody who isn't in possession of a residence permit. It's against the law.' (The clerk, it may be noted, was the head of a gang which sold stolen army petrol.) 'And we can't break the law, can we?' The clerk suddenly seemed to be very amused about something.

He was business-like again.

'Right. You get the permit, Clausen, and

I'll see what I can do for you.'

So it was Clausen, now, was it? he thought.

The clerk bent his head over his papers and with that the interview was terminated.

The other men looked up curiously when he got back.

'Papers. You know how it is,' he said briefly by way of explanation. He grabbed his cap and hurried away. In his hurry he forgot his sandwich. Later, when he was very hungry, he used to dream about that sandwich.

He waited all afternoon in the queue outside the Rathaus for a permit. He was not even within sight of the door when they closed that evening. The next morning he got there two hours before it was due to open and even then he was not the first. As he stood in the queue in the pleasant morning sunshine he thought of the play he had once read because it was banned. It was called 'The Captain of Koepenick' and it dealt in one scene with the ex-convict's attempts to get a permit because without it he can't get a job. But at the police station they won't give him a permit until he gets a job. A vicious circle. Then, he had thought it was funny, but now it wasn't so funny. But then, he thought, heartened by the sun, he didn't see why he shouldn't get a permit. He wasn't a criminal.

About midday he got inside and stood

73

there silently, with fifty other men, watching the clerks eating their sandwiches and chatting as if they weren't there. As the hand of the clock finally pointed to one, they languidly took their positions at the counter again, laughing and joking with one another.

When he finally reached the counter he asked for his permit.

The clerk poised his pen over the paper in front of him.

'Place of work?' he snapped.

'Well, that's a bit difficult. You see I have a … er had a job out at Billstedt … but,' he stuttered.

'Have you a job or haven't you?' the clerk asked dryly.

'No,' Clausen murmured, subdued.

The clerk hmmed.

'And where do you come from?'

'Schwarzenbek.'

'Well, why don't you go back to Schwarzenbek?'

'Because I've got no place to live there and … there are other personal reasons. Besides, I've got a job lined up here if I can get this damned permit.'

'None of that,' the clerk said, quite sharply. He breathed out heavily. He shook his head. 'Can't be done. There are too many of our own people to look after without…'

'But you don't come from Hamburg yourself,' Clausen interrupted him. 'I can tell it

74

from the way you speak.'

The clerk seemed not to hear and continued from where he had left off.

'There are too many of our own people to look after without having to look after outsiders. Besides, it isn't as if you were a genuine case of deportation or something like that from the Russian Zone. Next please!'

'But look here...' Clausen began and pounded his fist on the counter, enraged and desperate. Suddenly he was Leutnant Clausen, the old front-swine again.

The clerk was frightened for a moment. Then he raised his forefinger of his right hand at the man leaning against the wall at the back of the room. A moment later Clausen felt his hand seized from behind and jerked behind his back. He could not help screaming. Apathetically the waiting men made way for him to pass.

The clerk smiled wanly at the man in front of him and then he was his official self again.

'Next please.'

It was hard having to leave the old place again after living there together for nearly thirty-five years, but they could not stick living in the Russian Zone any longer. Even old women like mother weren't safe from them, were they? They decided to cross the border 'black'. That meant travelling as close as possible to the border and then crawling through the woods along the frontier in the Harz area at night. They were old, but they would try it.

There were six of them in the party that the guide was leading through the woods that night. He wanted more money, but they had no more to give. He insisted that they should give him the food that they had left in their rucksacks, but they refused. Then he left them. They decided to go on. It could not be much further to the frontier, they told themselves.

Over on the left the old man saw a flare go up. He knew what that meant from his days in the trenches in the First World War, but he did not say anything to his wife. As they were walking through a glade the moon came out and bathed it in a blue-white light. It was then that the machine-gun opened up and sent a stream of red and white tracer piercing through the night. They hit him in the first burst and he died straight away. Years before, when they had first married, she had always said that she would never survive him by three days. She did not. She was killed by the very same burst that killed her husband.

And they met each other, these two tough veterans who had been through hell to-gether. It was the first time since the prison cage in March.

'Hallo, old house. Still among the living?'

'Oh, my face! Hallo, you old stubble-hopper! What are you doing – spending the accumulated earnings of the last few glorious years?'

'Like hell! No, I'm flogging fags like the rest. That's the way to get the old green rags. What are you doing – getting down to the old Goethe again?'

'Ha, ha. You've got an idea! As a former member of the Armed S.S., I present a serious threat to society in general and democracy in particular if I develop myself intellectually. Accordingly, no study for me. No, I'm flogging stuff like you.'

'Fags?'

'Not likely. Nothing so plebeian! Petrol. That's the stuff to bring in the old marie. Know how much I made yesterday?'

'Am I Jesus?'

'Five thousand green rags. Not bad, eh?'

'It's better than having yer hand spat into. Ah, well, must blow. Have a big deal on.'

'Me, too.'

'Be seeing you. Tschuess.'

'Yes, sure. Mach's gut.'

So the two veterans parted to their very important engagements; two nineteen-year-old boys looking for cigarette ends in the gutter.

THE SERGEANT

The bunker towered up against the wretched background, its grey concrete mass spotted by small vents like the eyes of the blind. The sergeant followed the slow-moving grey mass inside. At the door the policeman asked him for his 'Ausweis' – his pass. He murmured 'foreigner' and the policeman waved him on. The Red Cross sister, standing next to the policeman, took him over. Deftly and unsmilingly she jerked the nozzle of the spray up each of his sleeves in turn and pumped disinfectant up in a white cloud. Then he had to open his jacket while she did the same to his armpits. Finally, she slipped the spray nozzle down the front of his trousers and squirted the stuff down his legs. He was deloused – the seventh time that week.

He opened his bundle and took out his mess-tin. He was given a pint of pea-soup and a hunk of black bread. Standing in one corner of the entrance-hall he had time to look around the bunker whilst he ate. The bunker was a former air-raid shelter, divided into a series of tiny cells, containing nothing but tiers and tiers of wooden bunks and here and there a table and a wooden bench. Here the people not only slept, but lived.

It was very warm in the bunker, but the

sergeant found that bearable. It was the stench that sickened him; it was like a thick wall of congealed bad breath. The people with him did not seem to notice the smell, however. They were too busy spooning up their soup out of their big army canteens. The sergeant looked at them over the top of his mess-tin as he held it up to his mouth. This was humanity pretty near its lowest, he thought. Life centred in a bowl of soup – even sex was forgotten.

It was during the night that he met the blind man. He tossed and turned on the bare wooden boards of his bunk, but he could not sleep for the heat and the stench. And all the time the raw light from the naked bulb glared down on the whitewashed walls. It made him feel that he had to get out in the fresh air or be smothered. He pulled on his boots hurriedly and grabbed his bundle. The policeman at the entrance murmured something about curfew, but the sergeant pretended not to understand and forced his way through. And it was then that he met the blind man.

He caught a glimpse of a black-pitted face in the yellow light that streamed out of the open door and then all was darkness again. He breathed in deeply, filling his lungs with the cool night air.

The figure next to him spoke:

'They wouldn't let me in after curfew.'

The sergeant remained silent.

'Why did you come out?' the voice asked.

'Nix versteh' – foreigner,' the sergeant said curtly, not wanting to continue the conversation.

'Where do you come from?'

'Oh – er – France,' the sergeant said wearily, wishing that the fellow would shut up.

'Oh, êtes-vous français? J'etais...'

The sergeant did not understand a word. He remained silent.

'You're not a Frenchman at all,' the voice in the darkness said quickly.

The sergeant lost patience.

'I'm an Englishman. Now, shut up!'

There was a long silence and the sergeant leaned against the concrete wall of the bunker and enjoyed the air. He might as well stay here until it grew light, he told himself. He had nowhere in particular to go, he thought, and laughed half-aloud.

'Why are you laughing?' the voice in the darkness asked.

'Because I have nowhere to go,' the sergeant said and laughed again.

'Because you have nowhere to go,' the voice repeated, puzzled. 'I have nowhere to go, but I don't laugh!'

'That's because you and me are two different persons,' the sergeant said.

'Why don't you go back to England?' the

voice asked, starting on a new tack.

'Why don't you go home?' the sergeant counter-questioned.

The voice was thin and wavering.

'I can't go home ... like I am.'

'What's the matter with you?' the sergeant asked, but received no reply.

It was next morning in the misty grey dawn that he discovered that his companion was blind.

'But you're blind,' he said brutally.

The blind man's face remained as immobile as the eyes sighted unseeingly on the heavens.

'How did it happen?' He did not wait for a reply. 'The war, like everything else,' he said bitterly. 'The human animal, with its thirst for power and might, destroying anything fine. It ought to be destroyed...'

'Don't say that,' the blind man interrupted. 'Surely we are something else than that.'

The sergeant laughed cynically.

'Name one way in which we are different! You should know better than I – with those blinded eyes.'

The blind man paled slightly under his blackened skin. The sergeant did not care. He ought to be made to realize how lousy the human race is, he told himself.

The sergeant undid his bundle and took out a piece of bread and started eating. After a few moments he tore a piece off and gave it to the blind man. They ate in silence. The sergeant finished and started to tie up his bundle again.

'Englishman,' the blind man said suddenly, 'take me with you.'

The request amused the sergeant.

'Where should I be taking you?' he asked. 'I'm going nowhere.'

The blind man persisted.

'But look here...' the sergeant began angrily, and then he was stopped suddenly by the look in the martyred eyes.

'All right,' he said, not knowing why he did so, 'come along. But I warn you. You'll not get very far with me.'

The blind man got to his feet and they set off down the road, the blind man with his head cocked on one side warily in the attitude of the newly blind. After they had gone some way, the blind man falling more and more behind, the sergeant went back and slipped his arm reluctantly through that of the blind man.

'Do you know?' the blind man said joyfully after a moment. 'This is the first time I've touched another human being since I came out of hospital months ago.'

'This is the first time I've touched another human being for years,' the sergeant said.

It was the soldiers who started it. A group of them went into the largest wine-store in town and broke into the cellars. They found thousands and thousands of bottles of cognac and the fell upon the flood of spirit. More soldiers – and officers too – came and they never left the cellars for two days, and when they did the trouble started. They invited the civilians to come and drink what they had left and the civilians tore the store to pieces – even the children rolled around the streets drunk. And then they went – a drunken, screaming, singing mob of soldiers and civilians – and broke into store after store. And they staggered about the streets in their coarse blouses and knee-boots and fired their automatics wildly into the air. And that day they raped even girls of seven.

But it did not stop there. When they had finished with the stores they started to break into private houses and steal from them. It was then that the Police Regiment was called in. It surrounded the town with its T.34 tanks and began to comb the ruined streets systematically. Anybody found looting – Russian or German – was shot on the spot. And the drunken soldiers, realizing that there was not much hope for them, dug themselves in in the ruins of the occupied city and began to fight back bitterly.

The blind man and the sergeant crouched in the ruins and listened to the rattle of small-arms fire all around them. They had been hiding in a cellar in the town for two nights now and had decided it was about time that they got out of it before it was too late.

The sergeant explained the position to the blind man.

'We're just at the side of a road,' he whispered, and almost put his arm out to point. 'At the far side there are some more ruins and beyond that woods. If we can get into the woods we'll be fairly safe. Now...'

'CRUMP!' the sound of a shell landing drowned the rest of his words.

'That must be one of the tanks,' he said.

The three Russians, who had been firing their automatics from a position further down the rubble, evidently thought so too. They started to clamber cautiously down to the edge of the road. Then with a wild shout they ran madly for the other side. A machine-gun opened up and one after another they skidded crazily to a stop and lay still in the middle of the road.

'CRUMP! CRUMP!'

There were more bangs and showers of stones flew into the air as more shells landed in the rubble. They're systematically shelling the area, the sergeant told himself.

'All right,' he shouted to his companion above the roar of the gunfire. 'It's about time that we went.'

Holding the blind man's hand tightly in his they clambered carefully down the pile of rubble to the edge of the road. At the end of the street – littered with empty bottles, rubble and paper – a tank was mounted on the pavement, its gun at the maximum elevation firing at the houses on the opposite side of the road.

'Right. Now listen,' he said tensely. 'When I've counted up to three I want you to run like hell for the other side of the road. We'll split up – smaller target that way. All right?'

The blind man nodded his head.

'One – two – three.'

And then they started running across the road. It seemed suddenly terribly wide and exposed to the sergeant. He heard the tick-tick of a machine-gun as he flung himself wildly into a pile of rubble at the other side. Wiping the sweat off his brow with his sleeve, he looked around for the blind man. To his horror he saw him jog-trotting up the road in the direction of the tank with bullets whipping up the earth all around him. For a moment the sergeant felt he was tied down to the ground by invisible bands and then he was out on the sun-baked road again running madly after the blind man, his body crouched almost double.

With a grunt he hurled himself into the blind man and knocked him with a thud to the ground.

'Grab a hold of my ankle,' he panted, his heart beating painfully.

The blind man groped until he found the sergeant's ankle. The sergeant started crawling wildly for the side of the road. A line of bullets kicked up showers of earth as they followed him persistently. He felt a burning sensation in his shoulder and then something hit his boot. With one last desperate effort he flung himself into the rubble, dragging the blind man after him. Then he collapsed.

CHAPTER III

JUNE

After a dog has had a love-affair, it puts on its hat, goes away and doesn't write.

Book on Dogs.

Many of them were going to look back on that summer as the best of their whole life. For five years they had concentrated their whole energies on getting there. Their whole existence had been dedicated to the task. And now they were there. They were a little tired and perhaps a little shaken still – every two in a hundred were pathological cases by now – but the sun came out and the girls wore their summer dresses.

For the first time in your life you were a rich man, who could afford to do what he wanted and could buy what he saw. You were a rich man if you had fifty cigarettes in your pocket that summer – a very rich man. Why, you bought a 'von' for ten cigs, that June, didn't you? And the beauty of it was that you could never go broke; free issue of fifty a week and seventy or so from the Naafi. Why, you were rolling in it, Jack!

87

'The war was just one big lark for the man in the street,' the corporal said, standing in front of them and blocking out the sun. He pronounced the words 'man in the street' as if they were slightly obscene. 'The petty clerk – the schoolteacher – the twopenny-'apenny commercial traveller – the bod. who wanted to get away from his missus for a bit. It gave 'em a chance to see new places' – and here the corporal grinned knowingly – 'and a chance to get into kipp with a fresh bint – and get stupid drunk on cheap beer.'

'What de yer know about that, Corp.? I thought you kept yersen pure in body and mind,' somebody interjected, but the corporal did not seem to hear.

'They got themselves nice cushy jobs in Antwerp and Brussels – and Echelon, and whipped the fags out of our Compo rations so that they could get their feet under the table with some bint and send home black-lace frillies for the little woman.'

The corporal looked down at the grinning men, who shaded their eyes against the sun.

'Four men in the line and eight at the rear to bring up char – that's our army for yer! You was the unlucky ones.' He drew his hands back and forth, as if he were rowing a boat. 'I'm all right. I'm in the boat, Jack, eh? You got yersen bashed into the Infantry. But you would have been the same as the others if you'd have had a chance. But yer weren't clever enough. Yer didn't have yer School Certificates.'

'What the hell's that?' somebody muttered, eager to learn.

'You, Charlie, fer instance,' the corporal went on. 'You'd have liked to have got yersen a nice cushy staff job in Antwerp, wouldn't yer? Nice clean uniform and plenty of fags in yer pockets. Flogging petrol to the Belgies. Plenty of bints and booze.'

Charlie grinned.

'Too damn Irish, I would! I'm not off me rocker like you.'

'Give it a rest, Corp.,' somebody else shouted. 'Yer making us cry. I'll be singing "Mother McCre" in a minute.'

The corporal frowned, but went on.

'You lot are the same as the rest. Wait till the Non-Frat ban comes. Like fiddler's elbows...'

The young soldier listened eagerly. He could see what the corp. was getting at. Well, he wasn't going to take advantage of a starving people, he told himself. They hadn't won the war for that. He was about to say aloud that he hated the flogging of fags in dark corners in the town, when Charlie shouted:

'Don't give us that bull about flogging! Go and tell that to the colonel with his fancy Mercedes and his blonde bit and the Service Corps officers who're flogging stuff by the lorry-load! You've seen the lorries with "Priority Loot" stuck in the window. That ain't no joke, you know.'

'Yes,' somebody else said. 'What's the harm in the ordinary bloke flogging a few fags? It was us that won the war, wasn't it?'

The corporal thought for a moment and they waited.

'Yes,' he said slowly. 'I suppose you're right there. But I'll tell you this. You blokes say yer cheesed-off now, but I bet in ten years' time yer'll be so sick of the little woman and the same old one-two-three that you'll be wishing that yer could be back here again … and…'

But the rest of the corporal's words were drowned in raspberries and jeers from the men. The corporal laughed, but did not say anything more and after a moment he went.

Charlie tapped his temple with his middle finger.

'That bloke's doolally,' he said. 'Too much sand when he was up the Blue.'

'More likely too much Red Biddy when he was in Glasgow,' somebody else said, and they laughed.

They lay back on the rough army blankets and let the hot sun beat down on their naked upper bodies. In the bright white light the muscles of their pale bodies seemed to dissolve into a soft flabbiness – like those of men relaxing after some strong physical and mental strain.

The young soldier, who had wanted to support the corporal, heard the sound of wooden heels on the pavement. He opened his eyes and raised himself on one elbow. A young blonde woman in a light short summer skirt was coming down the cobbled street. She had slim brown legs. As she passed the opening of one of the side-streets the breeze sent the light skirts billowing up above her knees. He watched her until she was out of sight. Then he picked up his shirt and went for his cigarettes.

'Hello, Fraulein, wo gehen duh hin?'

'I'm going walking.'

'Oh, you speak English.'

'Yes, I have studied it at school.'

'Oh, a high-school girl, eh?'

'Please?'

'You like to go spazieren with me in park?'

'I am not going spazieren with English soldiers in park.'

'Don't give me that! Do yer think I came in with the Banana boat?'

'Please?'

'You like chocolate?'

'Yes, I like chocolate very much. I like Hershey Chocolate. I like…'

'Well, I've only got this kind.'

'That is nice too.'

They went into the park. She walked ahead

slowly through the main streets and he followed a hundred yards or so behind until they were well out of sight of the M.P.s.

They sat on the grass. He had his arm around her.

'You jig-a-jig, Giselle?'

He clenched the biceps of one arm and slapped the palm of the other hand rapidly against it several times to illustrate what he meant. Giselle said nothing.

'You krank?'

'I am never ill since I was a baby.'

'No, I mean the other krank. I got cigarettes.'

The girl looked down at her torn shoes. The one and only pair she possessed.

They jig-a-jigged. He had promised her twenty cigarettes. He gave her ten.

'A high-school girl,' they laughed at the hospital when he told them. 'They're allus high-school girls or secretaries, son. But you'll learn…'

JIMMIE

The adjutant stood at the door with the interpreter and watched. After a cautious look to left and right the old man in the navy-blue peaked cap started to go through the ash-can. Now and again he found something and this he passed to the boy standing next to him with an open sack.

The adjutant could not contain himself.

'Come on,' he snapped to the interpreter.

They walked briskly over to the old man, who did not seem to notice them coming until the boy started tugging his sleeve.

'Hey, you!' the adjutant shouted. 'Stay where you are!'

He forgot that he was talking to a German, but the tone of his words had the desired effect. Old men do not register fear very well, and the old man's look of unconcern irritated the officer. He turned to the plumpish interpreter – a former major of the German Field Gendarmerie, who wore a pince-nez.

'Tell him, doesn't he know that he is committing a crime against the Occupation Forces when he steals out of an ash-can?'

'Yes, sir,' the interpreter said, and translated the officer's words.

The old man's look did not change, but the little boy with him began to cry bitterly. The adjutant's heart softened somewhat.

'Tell him, that I am going to let him off this time – for the sake of the boy. But it's the last time.'

The interpreter translated.

'Tell him that we in England are short of food, too, but we don't go searching in dustbins for it. We are too proud to do so. Why' – he warmed to his subject – 'my own wife has been without butter for days and has had to use margarine. But it doesn't mean that she went searching ash-tins.' He laughed at the thought. 'It just meant that she had to manage better. That's the whole secret of living in hard times – careful management. Tell him that.'

The officer stood silently and listened, as if he understood, whilst the interpreter translated his words. He was rather proud of the last bit about 'the whole secret'.

The interpreter finished. The old man was silent, but the little boy stopped crying and spoke. The officer stood rather impatiently whilst the boy's words were translated.

'The boy says,' the interpreter said, 'that they've had nothing to eat for two days. So they've had no chance to manage.'

'Oh, that's impossible,' the officer said. 'They get a fairly decent ration. A thousand calories a day – it's sufficient in this weather. When it's warm like this I often do without coffee and biscuits myself after lunch.'

'The boy says,' the interpreter gave the boy's reply, 'the ration has not been honoured this week or the week before that.'

The officer lost patience. To be seen arguing here in a back-alley with a dirty little German kid was not good for the dignity of an officer of the Occupation Forces. Besides, someone might think he was trying to get the boy. Some officers did these days with no law to punish them – there was that fat captain…

'Tell them that's enough,' he said irritably. 'I know on good authority – from a gentleman of the Military Government in the mess – that the ration is always honoured. Tell them to empty the sack back into the bin and be off.'

The interpreter nodded his head at every second word the officer said.

'You're quite right, sir, not to humour them,' he said. 'These are obvious survivals from the glorious days of the "Thousand Years Empire"' – his lips curled in a momentary sneer. 'The boy is obviously an example of the perfidious work of the Hitler Youth and the old man – a former S.A. man probably. And now they will not try to find a place in the new German democracy. They have become anti-social elements.'

Suddenly he remembered that he was not a politician but an interpreter. He translated the officer's words and added a warning of his own.

The two of them watched whilst the old man emptied the contents of his sack one by one back into the dust-bin: an empty tin of M. and V., with traces of meat and fat on the lid and a little gravy in the bottom, a handful of potato peelings, three large cabbage leaves and a blackened potato. This finished, the old man turned to the boy and held out his hand without saying a word. Reluctantly, the boy took a dirty piece of bread out of his jacket and handed it back to the old man who threw it after the rest into the bin.

'Got it this morning,' he said, by way of an explanation. 'The boy was saving it for to-night. Told him then he should have eaten it.'

But the officer did not understand a word.

The adjutant and the interpreter watched until the old man and the boy were out of the yard. The adjutant turned to the inter-preter and shook his head slowly.

'It's the greatest pity that the whole of the German nation is not as sensible and understanding as you, Schmidt,' he said. 'You see, the trouble with you – that is, the Germans as a whole – is that you have never learnt to think for yourselves. No initiative, you know.'

The officer paused. He knew that there was something else that they said about the Germans in that little book they had been issued with, but he had forgotten.

Schmidt permitted himself a fat smile.

'Thank you, sir,' he said. 'You are very kind. I do my best. I admit frankly I was like the rest. I was in the Party and all that. Though I think there were exceptional cir-cumstances in my case. But no matter. I realize that the democratic way is the best. We Germans must acknowledge our black past, the terrible crimes we have committed, and pay for them. Even the innocent ones

96

like myself – who only did their duty. Through suffering and hardship we will achieve that democratic ideal that is so finely embodied in the British nation. We must reject that philosophy which has chained the German intellect for the last hundred years – I might even say the last hundred and fifty years if one includes Fichte and...'

The word philosophy frightened the officer, whose only reading matter was the *Daily Express* during the week and the *News of the World* on a Sunday, and he interrupted: 'Yes, yes, I agree with you entirely.'

God, he thought, how these Huns do natter!

They went into the kitchen. The adjutant lifted up a pan-lid here and there and smelt the cooking food. He ran a thumb along the window-ledge for dust, but it was clean.

'Corporal!' he said to the corporal-cook standing by his side. 'Hands!'

'Sir!' the corporal said smartly and turned to the other members of the kitchen staff, and repeated: 'Hands!'

Charlie, Jimmie and the two maids lined up and held their hands out in front of them, palms downwards. The officer, followed by the cook and the interpreter, passed down the line. He started with Charlie, looking hard at his nails.

'Open!' he said, and Charlie opened his fingers so that the officer could see that there was no infection between them. 'Over!' the adjutant commanded. 'Right,' he said, and Charlie dropped his hands.

Jimmie tried to fix the officer with his eyes as he looked at his hands, but he did not succeed. He hated the whole business. It was like examining cattle at a market. He hated especially the Jerry interpreter, who followed the officer so officiously, as if he were part of the inspection. Typical, though, he thought. British officers always seem to get on best with their Jerry opposite number. No wonder the democratic element did not get a chance of taking part in the government.

The adjutant was satisfied. He nodded to the cook.

'All right, Corporal,' he said. 'And by the way. See to it that the Jerries don't go looking round the swill-bins and the dust-bin. They might start an infection with their dirty hands. You can never be too careful in this hot weather.'

'Sir,' the corporal said.

'Besides,' the officer continued. 'They get enough to eat. It's degrading for them if we give them a chance to come scavenging here.'

'Sir,' the corporal said again – the one word signifying his whole reaction to the situation.

'And, yes, you might let me have a look at the menu for tomorrow's Open Night.'

'Cream soup – yes. Vienna steak – plenty

of steak, Corporal. I managed to fiddle twelve pounds from the Echelon wallah. You'll be able to give everyone two pieces. Curry sauce – yes, the colonel likes that. But between me and you I don't know why. Peas, salad, *sauté* potatoes. Plenty of potatoes, Corporal. There are always plenty of those, aren't there?'

'Sir!'

'Good. Liqueur fruit salad. Savoury. Cheese and biscuits – and coffee.'

He handed the list back to the corporal.

'Very good, Corporal. Quite a nice meal. Nothing fancy, but quite nice.'

'Sir!' the corporal said.

With a last look round the kitchen the adjutant, followed by the interpreter, left.

Jimmie had been 'pearl-diving' – as they sometimes called washing-up in the army – since the war had ended; and he hated it. Charlie scraped the remains of the meal – the bacon-rind, the half-chewed piece of meat, the egg-shell used as an ash-tray – into the slops bucket and then handed the plate to him. He ducked it under the greasy water and swirled it around among the bits and pieces that Charlie had forgotten to remove. It was nauseating work; his hands always smelt of food as once they had always smelt of chocolate. Besides, the ever-present smell of cooking destroyed one's appetite after a time. Tonight Jimmie was on early turn and he was glad to be coming to the end of his shift. The swing doors, connecting the kitchen and the mess, swung open and Charlie came in. He pulled a long face and jerked an expressive thumb in the direction of the mess.

'That stumer Green's just blown in and wants some grub gildy. Have we anything left?'

Jimmie took his hands out of the greasy water and wiped them on the filthy tea-towel around his waist. His hands were white and wrinkled like those of a woman on wash-day. He went over to the hot-plate, where the food for late-comers was kept.

'There's some slingers and gippo,' he said. 'A few roast spuds and … er, plate of duff. Is that O.K?'

Charlie laughed.

'Are you kidding? Anything's good enough for them stumers.'

Obediently, Jimmie shovelled the roast potatoes on to the plate with the sausages and added the gravy. Charlie took the plate and spat into the gravy – as is the tradition in the kitchens of Officers' messes, being the one bit of disobedience the private soldier allowed himself – and carried it into the mess.

Jimmie hurried on with the plates, hardly caring whether he got the fat stains off or not. His mind was full of the problem of how to transcribe the scene around him into fiction. Charlie spitting in the gravy – he must remember that. What was it he usually said when he did it? Oh, yes, 'That'll put a bit of body into it.'

Charlie came back again. He flopped into the chair in the corner with his legs stretched out in front of him as if completely exhausted.

'Phew,' he said, wiping the sweat off his brow with his napkin. 'There, that's better. They've been running me off me plates, ternight, I can tell yer! I haven't even had time for a tab since seven. You got a fag on yer?'

Jimmie nodded in the direction of his battle-dress blouse, hanging on a nail on the wall.

'A packet of Woods in my pocket.'

Charlie got up and lit one of the cigarettes. He puffed out the smoke forcibly with a contented sound.

'Ta,' he said.

After a minute he spoke again. He lowered his voice confidentially.

'Jimmie,' he said, 'yer doing anything tonight?'

Jimmie did not say anything, and he went on:

'I've got one of them maids lined up and she's got a friend who'll come if you want.

You know – Giselle. The big one with… Any good to you?'

Jimmie shook his head, but did not turn round.

'Thanks, Charlie. I've got something else on myself tonight.'

'A bint?'

'No.'

'What, then?'

Jimmie hesitated a moment.

'Oh, a bit of writing I want to finish,' he said slowly.

'What – a letter?'

'No, not exactly. Something else.'

'Oh,' Charlie said, not knowing what to make of it. Men he knew did not turn down invitations like that. Still, he thought, Jimmie's always been queer ever since he got that bump on the head in Normandy.

'Well,' he said. 'If yer change yer mind, yer know where I'll be.' And, as an afterthought. 'Get it now, boy. You'll have plenty of time to write letters when yer sixty.'

'Thanks anyway,' Jimmie murmured.

'…around them is a starving people and yet they hold their parties and enjoy themselves as if starvation no longer existed in the world…' Jimmie wrote … 'A war has been won and the world is…'

No, he muttered, and scrubbed the sentence out. That's no good. It's far too obvious. People don't want their reading to be obvious. They want...

Up above he could hear voices in Charlie's room. In spite of himself he strained his ears, but he could not catch anything that was being said.

He licked his stub of pencil and began again.

'The officer licked the hot butter off his fingers – careful that no one in the mess saw him – and looked bored at the grey crowd of Germans that strolled past the large window.'

Above, he could hear the creak-creak of the bed springs. Charlie was on the job already. Savagely he threw his pencil down on the table. Breathing hard, he looked out of the window at the girls in their summer dresses, sauntering up and down the dusty road, waiting to be picked up.

He felt he had it in him to write – he knew he had it in him. He lacked education – he knew that – but he felt sure that the feeling he was putting into his book would make up for that. It was not just going to be a book about soldiers. It was going to include all those people down there with their joys and miseries. It was...

With an effort he jerked his eyes away from the window and made himself concentrate on the matter in hand. He took his pencil again and rolled the point between his pursed lips. Above his head the bed started to creak again. He cursed and grabbed his cap and belt. You've got to live life first before you can write about it, he told himself bitterly. He banged the door noisily behind him and the pencil rolled slowly down the white sheet of paper on to the floor.

He immersed himself in the crowds of soldiers and civilians who flocked the streets, although it was very near curfew time. Hardly conscious of the bricks and bomb rubble which littered the roads, he walked on, taking in the sights and sounds all around him. He stopped and watched a middle-aged man in German army uniform writing in chalk on the remaining wall of a bombed-out house.

'Seek my wife, Mrs Irma Gruen, nee Schurke. Last post from this address – 13.3.45.'

The man scribbled away vigorously and then grew self-conscious and stopped when he became aware of the eyes fixed on his back. Jimmie went on.

He passed a long row of hoardings, with the pictures of missing soldiers and civilians posted on it, and a crowd of men and women trying to make out the faces with the aid of matches in the half-light. There was something uncanny in the silent shuffle of the crowd from one hoarding to the next.

From over in the park he heard the sound

of accordion music. He went in that direction. A band of limbless ex-servicemen were playing Strauss waltzes, the best they could, for a crowd of drunken soldiers and screaming girls, who danced openly not caring about M.P. patrols. All the men in the little band had lost legs, and they played propped up on one crutch and wearing leather shorts, so that the crowd could see that they were really disabled.

Jimmie was sickened – yet fascinated – by the men's wounds. There was a queer cleaved look about the limb where the leg had been. There was one man whose leg had been amputated just beneath the knee, and the unfinished look of the limb chained Jimmie's eyes to it. He told himself that he ought to go on, yet he knew that he must stay and see everything. Everything must be seen and recorded. Everything.

Things were still bad when Jimmie left school in 1933, but he got a job with the 'firm' like most of the lads in his class. He was glad to be finished with school. At the time of the Scholarship examination, the sons of the clerks at the 'firm' got private tuition at night and went to the Grammar School. Nobody out of Hope Street, where he lived, did, except himself. But his old man would not let him take the place.

'We've got more to do with us brass than

waste it on thee, lad,' his father had said.
'Why, I was a half-timer with t' firm when I
was your age. Here's a meg. Go an' get
thasen an happorth o' kali.'

After that, it was marking time for three
years – going over the same stuff they had
done at eleven in Standard Five – with a bit
of history and geography thrown in.

'Now, all that marked on the map in red
belongs to us, boys. Imagine! One-fifth of
the world belongs to this tiny island!
Doesn't it make you proud?'

They had practical instruction, gardening
– no woodwork because the authority was
economizing after the expense 'of t' Prince's
Visit'.

'Now, you lads will be leaving school soon.
You'll be expected to put your back into it
when you join the firm, so you might as well
learn to do so whilst you're still at school' –
the headmaster speaking.

'Now, you, Jimmie. Get your hands in that
horse-muck and spread it around the
strawberries like I told you.'

Jimmie hesitates – he does not want to
touch the still warm stuff.

'Come on, lad! Get a hold of it. It won't
bite you! I don't know what you lads from
Hope Street are coming to. I didn't think
you were so particular about dirtying your
hands. From what I've seen of the place,
you wouldn't think so!'

Some of the kids laugh. Jimmie goes a deep red and hurriedly spreads the soft dark-brown strawy apples round the base of the strawberry plant.

In the firm they gave Jimmie the job of pushing a heavy iron bogie, laden with trays of chocolate, from one room to another. In the north, working-class lads do not grow very big, and working in the humid temperature necessary to keep chocolate soft enough for processing took it out of Jimmie that first year. He would get home in his overalls, which were brown and smelt strongly of chocolate – you could tell a man who worked for the firm anywhere because of the 'tangy' cocoa smell which engrained itself in his skin after a time – and collapse white and drawn on the bed.

But, for all that, Jimmie liked the work. His ma gave him five bob a week out of the twenty-five he earned for a shift of nine hours a day, five and a half days a week – and with five bob you could buy a lot in 1933. You could go to the pictures with the 'three-penny rush' on a Saturday afternoon when the cinema was packed full with a horde of screaming kids and youths watching cowboy films: Tim McCoy, Buck Jones – 'Look out, Buck, he's behind yer!'

You could go to dances at the Parish Hall on a Friday night for a tanner. A bare hall and a gramophone. A line of chairs at one

107

side for the 'lads': soaped hair that looked good at first, but which went white and flaky after a time, narrow, patent-leather shoes and white muffler. Jimmie bought himself a white 'art-silk' muffler with his first week's pay. A line of chairs at the other end with the 'lasses': bobbed hair – curled and singed at home with a poker heated over the gas-ring, flimsy shapeless dresses over dirty underclothes.

After the dance they took the girls home – whole gangs of them – and hung around the yellow light of the gas-lamp, joking and making fun of the girls until they broke up slowly into pairs – scared and tingling all over with excitement as they disappeared into the darkness of the lane.

For five bob you could buy yourself 'one of each' every night of the week: a penny-worth of chips and a twopenny fish.

'Gie's plenty of scraps, Missus!' you'd shout, and the woman behind the counter would cover the top of the chips with scraps of hard batter. After you'd eaten the lot, you would suck up the vinegar – softened by the fish fat – from the brown paper. Jimmie liked the meetings outside the fish shop best of all. It was good just to be with the lads, always dreading the raucous shriek from the darkness of the bottom of the street:

'Jimmie, are you gonna come home? Can't get yer out o' the bloody bed in t' morning and can't get yer in the bloody thing at night!'

Outside the fish shop you learnt how to say 'sweets' instead of 'chows' or 'goodies' because they were kids' words. You learnt how to say 'cop' instead of 'slop' because that was American and you were interested in American films. All that about sawn-off shotguns, molls and janes, stick-ups and the rest of it captured your imagination. It was there that you and the lads learnt to make up the doggerel verse which you wrote on the walls in chalk.

It's no use standing on the seat.
The crabs in – jump six feet.

Then later, as it grew nearer the time to go home, the conversation became more and more colourful and imaginative. They'd tell about the girls they'd 'felt' and what colour bloomers they wore. They'd tell about Mrs Sowerby down the street who was always inviting them into her house and offering them money if they'd do things for her. They'd tell about what Dad had done in the trenches in the last war. They'd tell how they would run away and join the Merchant Navy like Dick... And then would come the shout:

'Jimmie!' (or Peter, or Tommie) 'are you coming home this night? Can't get you out of bloody bed in the morning…'

They'd sneer under their breath so that the old woman could not hear.

'Aw, shut up, you old cowbag! That get thinks I'm still a kid.'

But the illusion was destroyed for that evening and the smell of chocolate-stained overalls would force its way into their consciousness again. After a few minutes they would break up and walk down the dark street, past the dust-bins ready for the morning collection, with the cats and rats already searching them for scraps. Jimmie would look at the stars twinkling in the night sky between the narrow confines of Hope Street and feel that he would explode if something did not happen soon.

When he was eighteen, Jimmie caught chocolate eczema. Everybody who worked in chocolate for any length of time caught it. His hands, bleached white like a woman's from the humidity of the Melange Room, were covered with scabs. He tried to hide them, but the foreman noticed and he had to report to the firm's doctor. He was given a week's notice.

'Occupational disease? Don't be absurd. These people are filthy. They come from filthy homes. They don't get the disease here, they bring it with them from their homes.'

There was a union in the factory, but the union organizer was paid jointly by the firm and the union. He was no good. He could do nothing. Anyway, what was the use of protesting? They gave you the boot at eighteen anyway. You were just cheap labour. At eighteen they had to give a five bob rise. So it was cheaper for them to sack you and take somebody fresh from school. There were always enough kids willing to go into the factory, although they knew what was in store for them at eighteen.

Jimmie did not mind being on the dole the first year, although his ma groaned like the devil. He would go ferreting occasionally with one of the lads, or help old Harbottle next door with his pigeons. Then, every dinner-time he would take his dad's dinner up to the factory and gossip with Charlie, the gate-keeper, about the Boer War and the King's Own Scottish Borderers. He also started reading; slowly at first because of the lack of practice, and then as many as six books a week.

The second year, when everybody seemed to be signing on, was not so pleasant. Everywhere you went you saw the drawn, yellow faces of the family men watching you: sitting on the step in collarless shirts looking at the dogs rutting in the gutter on a warm afternoon, standing outside the 'Exchange' in cloth caps and mufflers tied cross-wise over their throats waiting to draw their money, stubbornly sitting down on the edge of the pavement in the main shopping-streets, spitting dryly – waiting for the policeman to come along and move them.

In the evenings, Jimmie and the lads would drift down to the estuary and sit in silence on the dirty grass bank, looking at the sea and the far horizon, whilst the oily water lapped idly against the mud-banks of the shore.

In the winter of 1938 Jimmie got a job digging the bed for a canal lock – up to the waist in icy-cold water, eight hours a day in the middle of winter. On the strength of this he got married. At that time the only ones in the gang who had married were those who had been forced to. It was a matter of putting the girl 'up the pole' or 'in the pudden-club', as they expressed it, and being forced to the altar. Jimmie, however, had not touched his wife before they had married. For all he knew she might still be a virgin. She wasn't. All he wanted was to make a little secret world of his own and destroy the terrible openness of life at home.

They did not go on a honeymoon. In Hope Street they did not go in for that sort of thing. That was only for the people they read about in the *News of the World* on Sunday. Instead, they went on a cheap day-return to Saltburn one Sunday. They took sandwiches and bought a jug of tea on the sands. In the afternoon they were together for the first time in a field on the top of the cliffs. Jimmie had not wanted to spend the first night in the same bed that he'd shared with his brother ever since he could remember.

After that, love-making occupied the whole of his energies outside his work for the next few months. They had to live with his parents and the bed creaked, so they waited till everyone else went to sleep, or put a blanket on the floor and lay there. For a time he forgot everything that went on around him: his old man getting washed in front of the fire in the kitchen and all of them looking on; the afternoon his mother screamed when she was having another kid – he hated his father for that; the cheeky look in his brother's eyes when he complained of back-ache.

By the spring of 1939 he was out of work again. There was the first kid on the way. His wife started to grow fat and let herself go. Some mornings she didn't get up until twelve. He was used to hearing people about their most intimate toilet through the thin plaster-board walls of the house, but to hear his own wife make the same noises, as he lay on the bed and ran through the advertisements in the paper, made him feel sick.

Now, he just wanted to be alone. He would walk to the cross-roads just outside the town and watch the cars go by for hours on end, trying to imagine who the drivers were and where they were going. There were lads from the University, with great multi-coloured scarves around their necks like young blankets, and girls with their pretty legs sticking out of the dicky of a fast sports car. There were big business men in Daimlers and Rolls, already busy with their papers as they sped from one town to another. There were couples who looked as if they were going off for a dirty week-end, with the woman slumped well down in the seat so that no one could see her face. There were commercial travellers in the little Morrises with their jokes and free samples. Around these people Jimmie tried to build up little stories. But when he tried to put them down on paper, he found that what he'd written never seemed to convey what he'd thought.

His teeth started to go bad. When the pain got too much for him he went down to the Dental School and let them pull the tooth. They did it for nothing, but they treated their patients like stupid animals. His hands grew soft and white like those of a woman. A narrow, worried frown pinched his forehead. The veins in his legs stood out blue against the deadly white skin of his legs – the result of four years of bogie pushing. The muscles of his legs disappeared, and they appeared weak and spindly like those of old men. After the baby, his wife's breasts had sagged and she had grown sloppier and lazier than before. Gradually, all desire for her began to disappear.

At twenty, Jimmie felt like an old man. When he was called up for the army in October 1939, he felt himself years older than the eager young men who surrounded him in the barracks – full of blow with their pin-ups and Brylcreemed hair.

The army made him strong again. He was glad to go overseas in 1940 so that he no longer had to face the prospect of going home on leave again to Hope Street. The new places and new faces gave him a certain amount of the intellectual and spiritual nourishment that he needed. He started his little word sketches again when he was in hospital in Bayeaux in 1944 after being wounded, and sold a short story to a magazine. He could not cash the cheque they sent him, but that did not matter. He knew now what he was going to do when he was finished with the army. England, home and beauty had had him, he told himself. He owed it nothing. He was going to stay over here and write and write.

Jimmie's eyes hurt from tiredness and the bright light of the mess. He felt mesmerized as he stood there and watched dully as the officers played. It was the weekly 'Open Night' at the mess, when the officers invited the ladies from the hospital and the local UNRRA unit for a drinking session to be followed by horse play. The horse play was now in progress. They had already wrestled in a heap on the floor, and the female lieutenant from the hospital had had her skirt torn off by the colonel with the itchy fingers, who had accompanied her outside, still apologizing, and had not come back yet, although the incident had happened some fifteen minutes ago. They had already set fire to handkerchiefs in each other's pockets and given the orderly officer, young Sims, a glass filled to the top with gin and lime instead of the lemonade he had ordered. He was now outside, spewing his guts up. And now they were racing. Six officers, each with a lady on his back showing a liberal amount of flesh, were nosing peas down the length of the room. The peas made the race last longer, and gave the spectators a good look up the ladies' skirts.

Everybody was shouting wildly, waving their glasses in the air to urge on the crawling officers. The ladies, catching the mood of the spectators, dug their heels savagely into the ribs of their mounts, as if they were riding real horses. For a moment Jimmie wondered what it must be like to have those scented, silken legs gripped tight around

116

your back. It gave him a kick. In his excitement, a young officer knocked over a vase of flowers, and the water from the upturned vase poured over a pile of some sixty chicken sandwiches. Jimmie flashed a look of disgust in his direction, but the officer just grinned foolishly and made no attempt to pick the vase up. Sixty wasted chicken sandwiches, Jimmie thought, and the bastard does not do anything but grin, although he can see men and women searching dust-bins for food any day of the week.

He was about to go across and pick up the vase, when he heard a voice behind him say:

'Waiter, another whisky!'

He turned round quickly. It was Lieutenant Green. He fetched the drink and placed it in front of the officer, who was sitting by himself – the table in front of him covered with empty glasses. Green signed the chitty for the drink with an unsteady hand, but did not give it back to Jimmie. Instead, he looked at him for a long second and said:

'What the hell were you looking at that officer like that for just now?' His speech was slightly slurred.

'I beg your pardon, sir,' Jimmie stuttered. 'I don't know what you mean exactly.'

'Don't give me that bull,' Green said bitterly. 'I know you men. Some of you get away with murder. Give you too much meat and you start getting big ideas. Be a good job when some of you are back on the dole.'

Jimmie was flabbergasted. The suddenness of the attack overwhelmed him. Before tonight he had probably only exchanged half a dozen words with Green in the last month. He began to stutter something, but Green interrupted him.

'I'm sick of the lot of you with your damn fish and chip world. You'd think these days that only the person who lives on five pounds a week and spends his time queuing in a dirty raincoat and a cloth cap was worth bothering about. Your lot are making everybody as dull as themselves. But I'll tell you this gratis – do you know what that means?'

Jimmie nodded his head, suddenly very cool, but he did not say anything.

'Well, it surprises me,' Green said. 'Anyway, I'll tell you this. You'll regret it when you get rid of us for good. You'll be so damn bored that you'll start cutting each other's throats just for something to do – like you do now when you've swilled enough beer in your filthy Naafis.'

He paused for breath and looked up at Jimmie through narrowed eyes. Suddenly he seemed very sober.

'You hate our guts, don't you?' he said vehemently. 'Come on and admit it! If you had your way me and my kind would be hanging up from the nearest lamp-post now.

Well, come on – admit it. I won't put you on a charge.'

'I think you've had to much to drink, sir,' Jimmie said softly.

He hated himself for saying it. He knew he sounded like the faithful old retainer. He ought to have bashed in Green's face. There was a silence and the noise of the room seemed far off in the background. Suddenly the tension was broken and Green gave him the chitty. He smiled, and Jimmie smiled back politely. He went back to his position at the back of the room.

The race had ended, and the winner was buying a round of drinks for everybody at the bar. Jimmie thought of what Green had said. The stupid b. is too drunk to know what he says, he told himself. His thoughts trailed away and he found himself listening to the babble of voices around him.

…'Riddled with it – these Jerry women, you know. Wouldn't touch one of 'em with a barge pole…'

'Old Bill Davies, at H.Q. got it, you know.'

'Go on!'

'Pukka.'

'Reminds me of the time I was coming down to Alex. on a spot of leave from up the Blue…'

'This Hun chap was standing behind me like a positive hawk. Really he was. After my

119

fag-end, of course. I smoked on, pretending I hadn't noticed him – as if you can't smell a Hun a mile away! Anyway, when I finished it, I dropped it in the gutter and took a couple of steps backwards. He was there like a shot, bending to pick it up. Then I – you'll scream – I put my foot on it and positively ground it to nothing in front of him. You should have seen the look on his face. I nearly bust a gut laughing.'

'And this shocking great tank came up and me and old Pongo pretended to be dead. It stopped – only about shocking five yards away from us – and the crew got out and began to shocking well brew up. I looked at old Pongo and he looked at me, and then I whispered to him to get ready to shocking well run for it and got a shocking grenade…'

'I do think the tango is a positively randy dance, don't you?'
'Yes, you're right. It certainly does do something to the inner man.'

'I don't think I could wish for a better husband than George. He's so dependable.'
'No, I don't suppose you can really. Working in the bank and all that. And I know I couldn't wish for a better wife than Clara. She really is a decent type. But I'll be frank with you. I mean, I love my wife – I hate that

word, but you know what I mean – but all the same a man likes a change. You know, a slice off the same old...'

'Yes, I appreciate that. I think it applies to some women, too. I always say there are two types of men – lovers and good husbands. George belongs to the latter category. Decent – solid, you know. He never attracted me – er ... sexually.'

'Hm. And me – what category do I belong to?'

'Well, I couldn't say ... yet!'

'Shall we go upstairs and ... see my etchings?'

They laughed.

'Did you see the little German girl with the scabs on her legs?'

'Yes – must have been the size of a shilling at least!'

'Shocking, what?'

'Wonder what it is?'

'They say it comes from undernourishment.'

'Oh, I don't know, old man. Shouldn't think so. They get enough to eat, I read somewhere in the paper. It's probably due to their laziness. I saw at least ten Jerries today who could have done with a shave. Not the same as they were in the Desert. Must have gone to pieces, what?'

'Yes, I suppose they must. Oh, do have

another grape.'

'No, I don't feel any animosity towards them. Why, I even spoke to a German yesterday.'
'Pretty decent of you, but, I mean, how do you manage in your job in the Military Government, if you don't usually speak with them?'
'Well, usually I just send them little notes through my interpreter chap.'

'We have our exits and entrances, and not many of them. Everything's been tried, I suppose.'

'I often wondered how they thought we would win the war through mass prayer to the Almighty. The Jerries would win every time. They'd outpray us – two to one.'

'Treat 'em like the wogs in India. We're too soft on 'em. Give 'em plenty of the big stick, I say. A good turn-out – a smart soldier – that's the only thing they respect. If one of them is introduced to you don't offer him your hand or stand up – bad form, you know. The Russkies are the fellows who know how to deal with 'em. Not soft like us. Give 'em plenty of the big stick, I say...'

Jimmie could not stick the atmosphere of the

mess any longer. They had dimmed the lights for a more intimate form of dancing. So, with a cautious look around him, he went.

Outside, he breathed in the fresh night air in huge gulps. He ripped open the front of his tunic and let the cool air play on his heated body. For a long minute he looked at the night sky, sparkling with stars, and was about to go to his room when he saw something move in the shadows of the yard. His hand went into his pocket and brought out the tiny Italian automatic he had looted some two months before. His eyes strained to penetrate the darkness. Yes! There was something moving in the region of the dust-bins. He could see the outline of somebody leaning over one of them. He levelled the pistol and spoke in broken German.

'Hey! What you do there?'

The lid of the dust-bin clanged down noisily in the silence of the night, but there was no reply.

He challenged again. The figure spoke.

'I was only looking for a bit of bread.' It was the voice of a woman – a young woman.

'Come here,' he said, and then, as the woman came closer: 'Are you hungry?'

'Yes,' the voice replied simply.

Then he had an idea. Let like and like stick together, he told himself.

'I can give you all the food you want,' he said.

The woman did not reply, but he led her into the kitchen.

'I cannot turn the light on,' he whispered, 'because of the officers…' He did not know what the German for 'next door' was, so he left it at that.

He heaped a plate in the dark with the best he could find. There was some white meat of chicken, a cold chop, potatoes and a half-tin of peaches. She ate everything he gave her without a word. He did not say anything whilst she ate, but just sat there and waited. He fumbled for her hand in the darkness – it was cold and thin – and placed a glass of milk in it.

After she could not eat any more, she spoke.

'You want me to stay, Tommie?' Her voice was different than before. It had a forced sensuousness about it – yet it wasn't that of a pro., Jimmie thought.

Jimmie reflected a moment in the darkness, his face masked from her. He knew if he let her go now he would not be able to sleep, regretting the lost opportunity. Then he remembered what Green had said.

'No,' he said. 'You can go. You do not need to…' he did not know word for 'pay', so he said … 'give me for the food. I give it gladly.'

He saw her out to the gate. She stopped as if she were about to say something, but no words came. Then she was gone. Jimmie stood there a long time looking after her. He had not seen the girl's face – didn't even know her name – but he knew he would remember her and that night.

ILKA HARMANN
Ilka Harmann walked away slowly into the darkness, trying to comprehend the motives of the unknown soldier. Why should he, a former enemy, give her something for nothing? Perhaps, she thought, he had wanted something in return and she had not understood.

A month ago she would have taken anything given to her in the spirit it was given, not anticipating any ulterior motive. But in the last month a lot of things had happened to her. On the way to the border a man in a car had picked her up. He was quite old, she thought.

'I'm in my best years, my dear,' he had begun, and launched into a detailed description of his prowess the night before with another woman he had picked up on the Autobahn. When he stopped the car that night, he took it for granted that she would sleep with him. When she refused, he thought it was because of his age and began to protest.

'But my dear,' he said, 'I'm every bit as good as a man of thirty. Last night I must have ... always tried to keep myself fit ... swimming in winter, sport clubs...'

She refused again, and he tried to force her. When she started to scream, he dropped his cultured accent and snarled:

'Go to the devil then, and get out of my car. Wait till the Russkies get their big paws on you! They won't be so considerate – and a good job, too!'

Seven days later she arrived in Hamburg after walking the rest of the way. She tried to get a job and was unsuccessful. But she seemed to have acquired new strength. She was determined not to let herself go like the other girls in the bunker, who lived off Red Cross charity and what they could earn going with soldiers. She took stock of herself. She did not know anything. She had not needed to with a father who owned two hundred acres of land. She decided she would become a waitress or a barmaid. There, at least, you had access to food. But her clothes were against her, she realized, bloodied and dirty as they were. Next morning, she found a lonely spot up the estuary and slipped out of her dress. She washed it with the rest of her soap and sat the rest of the day in the sun whilst it dried. Towards evening she put it on again and finished drying it off on her body. That way it did not crease too badly.

She found the place they had told her

about at the labour office. It was out at St Pauli – the brothel area – though she did not know that then. She went down the stairs into the dimly lit café and through the tiled corridor to the manager's office. She knocked and went in.

The manager sat behind a desk which was far too big for the room. He was quite a young man, but very fat. In front of him were the remains of his breakfast: a greasy, fat-hardened plate with the yellow traces of egg and one or two uneaten cubes of German bacon, the empty skin of a sausage, a jammy knife and an eggshell, which was being used as an ash-tray for his cigar.

He did not offer her a seat, but kept her standing there whilst he looked her up and down with a critical eye.

'So yer want a job,' he grunted. 'Well, yer'll certainly earn enough green rags if you work for me. Some of my girls knock up as much as thirty and forty fags a night. And that's money, I can tell you!' He said this with a certain amount of pride.

'Hm,' he said, as if engrossed in some problem. 'What are yer round the upper storey?' he tapped his chest. 'The bust.'

She blushed furiously.

'What exactly do you…' she began.

'Customers like to see a bit of meat,' he said shortly, anticipating her.

'Thirty-six,' she whispered.

He nodded, seemingly pleased.

'Fine, but get it up a bit more, will you? Always knock 'em in the eye, if yer can. Let you have a good bra for ten fags if you want. Can get 'em in black, too. Let's have a look at yer pins.'

She was puzzled.

'Yer legs,' he said. 'Yer legs.'

She thought of the girls sitting dirty and apathetic in the bunker under the glaring light of the naked bulb and raised her skirt slowly above her knees. The manager looked at them for a long time – or so it seemed to her – sucking at his teeth, seemingly trying to remove a piece of food lodged in some cavity.

'Nearer,' he commanded, gesturing with one hand.

She did so, her skirt still held high.

He put a flabby, sweaty hand on her leg just above the knee. She tensed, but did not move away.

'All right,' he said, keeping his hand on her knee. 'You'll do. Start tomorrow at six. Hundred and fifty a month. One meal at eleven and all tips.'

She waited for him to take his hand away, and after a moment he did so. Later, she found out he was queer, so she need not have worried. She left. She was learning.

In the next few days she learnt a lot more. She learnt how to smile when the fat black marketers and the profiteers pinched her bottom as she moved between the tables. She learnt how to roll her eyes and look longingly so that the customer would buy another bottle of the raw spirit that they made in the basement from potatoes. She learnt how to give Jonni, the bouncer, the wink when the customer ran out of money and started complaining of being bilked. She learnt.

One night a rich farmer was ushered in as if he were a king. Everything he possessed seemed to have belonged to someone else before he had got his big paws on it.

'See this ring,' he would say as she passed him. 'Got it off a count for a dozen eggs. Good business, eh?' And he would laugh drunkenly.

Or:

'See these pearl studs? Got them off a soldier who said they had once belonged to a Russian duke. Not bad for a fellow who was born plain Gier, eh? Got 'em for a side of bacon. We farmers ain't the country yokels you townsfolk think we are.'

They kept the place open for him until he was the only customer, and still he went on spending his money like water. When he finally decided to leave, he wanted to take her with him. He called her over and took something from his pocket.

'Here,' he said cunningly. 'You be good to

me tonight, young lady, and you can have this.' He dangled a gold watch in front of her by the strap. 'Got it from a lady and...' a thought struck him and he laughed ... 'and something else besides. But that's another story.'

When she refused, he called over the manager. He pushed the pretty young waiter, with whom he slept, to one side and shook his fist threateningly under her nose.

'I ought to stick one on you for this,' he said, his pasty face flushed unhealthily. 'Go with the man,' he hissed. 'He's got plenty of marie. He'll see that you live like God in France if you please.'

Again she refused. He fired her on the spot. When she left that night, Gier was sitting with his arm round the pretty young waiter, whilst the manager looked on gloomily.

And now she was out of a job again. Well, she told herself, as she stretched herself out on the grass of the park, at least I've got a good meal in my stomach. Tomorrow's always another day. Today red, morning dead. She turned on one side and fell asleep. She had not learned yet.

'Razzia!' they shouted, and panicked. 'A raid!'

Some of the soldiers let themselves be pulled by their girls towards the gates of the park, but most of them just relinquished their hold and let the girls run for it.

The M.P.s drove their jeeps through the gates and jumped out, followed by the green-uniformed German police, who had to leave their vehicle outside. Quickly they spread out – the German police with rubber truncheons in their hands – and drove the girls into one corner of the park. Some of the more hardened cases, who had been through it all before, just waited there cynically, but here and there one could see a girl struggling desperately in the arms of a hefty military policeman. They finally collected some fifty or so girls in a circle, and a solitary soldier who had started to protest when his girl had been seized. Then they began to go through the girls' papers. Those whose papers were not in order were herded into an open truck outside the gate; there were twenty in all.

Within ten minutes of the disappearance of the police, the park was full of strolling soldiers and girls again. It was as if there had been a shower of rain which had now cleared up.

Inside the bare ice-cold hall – in spite of the blazing sun outside – the girls shivered as they stood there naked, waiting. The English army doctor wore surgical gloves, but he did not do anything about sterilizing them after he had touched one woman and had moved on to the next.

'You sick?'

'No.'

'Sit on that and get your legs up.'

He used his instrument and gave the smear to the orderly, who looked at the slide underneath the microscope.

'Next! You sick?'

'No.'

'Sit on that and get your legs up.'

Once the doctor's face lost its bored, professional look.

'Corporal,' he said, and the young R.A.M.C. corporal left his microscope and came across.

The doctor pointed his finger at the woman's breast.

'That's interesting,' he said.

'Yes, it is quite interesting,' the corporal agreed, looking hard at the woman's breast. 'I suppose you mean the nipple, sir?'

'Good man,' the doctor said heartily. 'I can see we'll make a doctor out of you yet before you're demobbed. Yes, the nipple is quite revealing. Just feel the case of the breast and see.'

Rather gingerly, the young corporal put his hand on the woman's left breast.

'A little more firmly,' the doctor advised. 'Yes, that's the way.'

'Well?' the doctor said.

'Yes, I think so, sir,' the corporal answered. 'At least, it feels like it. What shall we do about it, sir?'

'Nothing to do with us, old boy,' the doctor said, suddenly bored. 'Not our pigeon. Let somebody else worry about that.'

The woman somehow sensed the meaning of the conversation between the two men, and she began to cry softly, holding her hand to her eyes for want of a handkerchief. The doctor flicked a look at her disinterestedly.

'Next! You sick?'

'No.'

'Sit on that and...'

They found two were positive – one was the woman with cancer.

'In the Feldlazarett we had been expecting the Amis to come for weeks. One bright June morning they did so. About eight o'clock a small convoy of troop carriers came through the gate and grinded to a stop in the courtyard. Two soldiers with carbines dropped off and ran to the gate. Another two ran to guard the main entrance. Then, led by a young lieutenant, with the blue and silver combat badge on his chest, they entered the building noiselessly in their rubber boots. That was perhaps the unreal part of it. If they had come stamping in in hobnails it would have somehow lent reality to the scene, but they came in softly – with that sensuous glide from the waist which seems peculiar to the Americans. I wonder if it has anything to do with the mixture of negro blood?

'But I mustn't digress, must I?

'As I say, we had been expecting it, but not as bad as it actually was. The fellow in number eight, with the wound in his stomach, who started screaming if you came within ten feet of him because of the vibration – they took him. Schwester Leni protested, but they shoved her against the wall and she began to cry. It was rather funny in a way, too. Obersturmbannfuehrer Nicholai, who had been boasting with all his decorations on his chest, tried to hide in the linen closet, but they dragged him out.

'The kitchen-bulls, the ward creeps – all the S.S. men – they took them away. They ripped the transfusion bottles from above them and released the limb pulleys. They took the drainage tube out of that fellow with the lung wound I told you about, and the stink nearly gassed us. And, worst of all, they took that burnt chap – Wolf-Bodo Hinkermann – out of the saline bath. God, I wouldn't like to see anything like that again.

'Within half an hour there wasn't a S.S. man in the place. Gracious Lady. The Americans call it "hustle" in their language. Oh, thank you. I wouldn't say no to another cup.

'Oh, yes, some.'

'Ten in all on the journey, I heard. And then a couple died afterwards in hospital.

'The burnt chap? Couldn't say.'

THE INTERPRETER

Erich Mathiessen got out of bed carefully in order not to wake his wife, who lay sleeping by his side. He went over to the table and lit the oil-lamp. By its light he could see that it was already half-past three. Time, he thought, and began to dress slowly, pulling his clothes on with an occasional grunt.

He washed and began to pack his rucksack with the food that lay neatly piled up on the table. There were ten pounds of potatoes, for which his wife had worked a whole day. There were ten cigarettes and a loaf of bread, which she had saved from her ration. And there was a pile of fruit, for which she had had to tolerate Gier's fingers on her, trying to force their way up her skirt. The food on the table had cost her a week of misery and pain, though she had not told him that.

'Come on,' Gier used to urge when he caught her alone in the barn or in the fields. 'We can always do it without his knowing. Think of what I can give you – eggs and steak and everything.' And he would lay his fat sausage fingers on her and she would tolerate it.

He would ask her to come to his room at night. She would refuse and he would smile his sour smile and say nothing. And at night she would pray: Please God, let Erich take me away from here. Please God, let Erich take me away from here. But Mathiessen knew nothing of this.

'There's always work for a man who wants to work,' he had said the night before. 'Where there's a will there's a way.'

'But Erich,' she had pleaded. 'Can't you get a job out here?'

He had laughed and pressed her hand hard.

'What could I do out here with these swede-bashers? I'd only be wasted. No, it's back to the city for me.'

He had seen the look of concern on her face.

'Don't worry,' he had said. 'I'll be back in two weeks' time. Just you see.'

'Don't leave me,' she had whispered, and lowered her head. 'Don't leave me.'

As Mathiessen moved around the room, he placed his feet very carefully so that he did not disturb her sleep. He felt happy for all the early hour. This time he knew he would get a job in town. He knew.

His wife stirred in her sleep uneasily, and he looked at her tenderly. A sudden feeling of compassion swept over him, and he went over to the bed and kissed her on the forehead. She woke up, startled.

'I'm going now, darling,' he said. 'It's

nearly four.'

She started up, surprised.

'I didn't hear the alarm,' she said apologetically.

He restrained her gently.

'It's all right. I'm not very hungry.'

'But you must have something warm to drink before you go. It's such a long journey in the train. We...'

He smiled, and stroked her forehead gently.

'Don't worry,' he said, and tried to smooth the frowns out. 'Don't worry.'

The village clock chimed four. He counted the strokes aloud. He got up from the bed.

'I must go now,' he said. 'It's time.'

She clutched hold of his hand.

'Gier,' she began, and then stopped suddenly.

He waited for her to finish her sentence, and he laughed when she did not.

'All his interests are in his trousers,' he said, and released himself gently from her grip.

'Goodbye,' he said from the door. 'Be seeing you soon – and this time with a job.'

She did not say anything, and he closed the door.

Outside it was cold, and he shivered. He walked down the deserted village streets – bright in the moonlight – and began to whistle. He felt good. He knew it in his bones that this time he would be lucky.

'The next time I'm here,' he said aloud to the empty street, 'I'll be a member of the great working classes.'

The train took ten hours to crawl the distance of some hundred kilometres from the village to the city, and it was already well into the afternoon when they arrived in the main station. The train came to a stop with a jerk, and the people began to pour out, bent under the heavy packs of food that they had brought back from their trips 'overland' – as they called their search for food from the farmers. They had stood day in, day out, outside the farmer's backdoor, with the dogs snapping and barking at their heels, whilst the farmer treated them like dirt. They had been humble and respectful, and had been thankful when they had been given a yellowed cabbage or handful of maize. And now they were home again, and eager to get off the platform.

Suddenly, the loudspeakers boomed out mechanically over the noise of hurrying feet. It came through in four languages:

'This is a search! This is a search! Everyone will remain standing where they are now. This is a search!'

Mathiessen opened his rucksack. Carefully, he laid the fruit, bread and cigarettes on the clean napkin that his wife had given him the night before. Then the police were among them in their green uniforms, accompanied by an English officer and a man in civilian clothes.

The man in mufti stopped in front of Mathiessen.

'What yer got?' he said thickly.

Mathiessen pointed to the food laid out at his feet, but the man in mufti did not look down.

'I said, what have you got?' he said. 'Must I repeat myself again?'

'I've fruit, potatoes, bread and cigarettes,' Mathiessen said. 'My wife saved it out of her ration.'

'Sir!' the man said. 'You forgot the "sir".'

'Sir,' Mathiessen forced the word. What does it matter? he told himself. No trouble now.

The man surveyed Mathiessen with his piggy eyes behind the pince-nez. When he opened his mouth, Mathiessen could smell cognac.

The English officer strolled up, swinging his cane as he walked through the crowd of Germans – the people making a path for him. The officer looked bored.

'Find anything, Schmidt?' he asked uninterestedly.

'Another hoarder, sir,' the interpreter said smartly, proud to be able to display his English in front of the crowd. 'Fruit, bread, potatoes and cigarettes. Says it's a present from his wife.'

'Hm,' the officer said. 'What's the drill now? It's the first time I've been on one of these stunts.'

'Confiscation, sir, and a warning.'

'O.K.,' the officer said jauntily. 'I'll leave it to you and the law.'

He inclined his head slightly and walked away.

Mathiessen tried to contain himself as the two men spoke together in the foreign tongue. He felt himself humiliated, in the way a patient must be when his doctors discuss him at his bedside whilst the students look on. Hold it in, he told himself. Hold it in. Think of the job.

Schmidt touched one of the apples with the toe of his well-polished shoe.

'What did you give for these?' he said. 'Your watch, or what?'

'I tell you that they are what my wife saved from the ration,' Mathiessen began.

But the man gave the apple a light tap with his toe, and it and the other fruit began to roll down the dirty platform. Somebody stepped back and squashed one of the big soft apples to pulp in the dirt. (The apples for which Mathiessen's wife had tolerated the fat fingers of Farmer Gier on her body.)

Mathiessen flushed deep red and he clenched his fists hard, but after a moment he bent down and began to gather up the fruit from beneath the feet of the people standing around.

He looked up from where he bent.

'You shouldn't have done that, sir,' he said mildly. 'You shouldn't have done that.'

Schmidt sneered and turned to one of the green-clad policemen.

'Confiscate that fruit!' he snapped.

'I won't have anything to eat if you do that,' Mathiessen said hollowly, his eyes glazed over as he looked up again. 'And hunger hurts. I know that from experience.'

'Experience,' Schmidt sneered. 'What kind of experience could a poor fish like you have?'

He bellowed at the green-clad policeman again.

'Confiscate that muck! Confiscate it – quick!'

With a vicious, well-aimed kick he knocked the rucksack over on its back, sending the potatoes rolling over the platform and down on to the lines. (For these potatoes Mathiessen's wife had worked for ten hours in the fields under the blazing sun singling the young plants, until her hands were torn and bloody all over from the thistles and thorns which grew there.)

It was then that Mathiessen hit Schmidt. The blow caught him off his guard, and he staggered back, his hands clasped over his stomach, gulping desperately for air.

141

They hit him in the ribs and tore at his arms and, when he lay unconscious on the cold concrete of the platform, they kicked him in the ribs. And they dragged him away and put him in the 'Green Minna'. And he did not come home again to his wife, and one day Gier seduced her in the hay, and after a time she became pregnant and he put her out.

And when he had been taken away, the two children sat down contentedly on the cold concrete and clawed up the squashed fruit from the platform with their stiff fingers. They ate the fruit greedily and when they left there were only the wet stains still visible on the platform.

He came out, grins all over his face.
    'Well?' we asked.
    He winked.
    'You know me, boys.'
    'What did yer give her for it?'
    'Corned beef as usual.'
    'How do yer do it? I tried a whole week with that bint.'
    He winked.
    'I could have had her old man for a tin of spam.'

CHAPTER IV

JULY

Mitgegangen, mitgefangen, mitgehangen.
(Ganged together, caught together, hanged
together.)

Old German Saying

GREEN
Green sat down at the table outside the café
without asking her whether the chair were
free or not. She was a very pretty girl, but
that did not matter much.

He sat there quietly, and let the hot sun
beat down on his face for a moment, then
he took a bottle out of his pocket and put it
down on the table.

'Like a drink?' he asked the girl in
German.

'O.K.,' she said, in no way surprised to
hear him speak the language.

He clicked his fingers at the waiter.

'Two glasses and a corkscrew, Herr Ober!'

'You'll have to pay cork money,' the waiter
said.

'How much?'

'Two cigarettes, sir.'

143

Green put five loose cigarettes on the table. The waiter's yellow face flushed slightly.

'Thank you, sir,' he said, emphasizing the 'you'.

Green let the waiter open the bottle of whisky, but he poured the drinks himself.

'Hals und Beinbruch,' the girl said, raising the glass in toast.

'What's that mean?' he asked. 'I've never heard that one before.'

'Literally, it means "neck and leg break". But I suppose you might translate it into English as "happy landings".'

'Oh, you speak English,' he said shortly.

She nodded.

'Ah well, happy landings!'

They had another drink and another. The evening shadows began to lengthen and the heat of the sun gave way.

'What time is it?' she asked suddenly. 'I sold my watch on the Black Market yesterday.'

'Getting on for eight.'

'Hm. Not much longer to curfew.'

They sat in silence for a few minutes and watched the people go by. A boy bent between the tables and picked up a cigarette end that Green had dropped.

'You sick?' Green asked, resuming the conversation.

'How do you mean, sick?' She pointed to

the region of her head. 'Up there, do you mean?'

'I suppose so,' he said.

She shrugged her shoulders.

'Don't know.'

They stopped talking and watched a young girl pass in a dress with a pink stain on the back. It looked as if it had been scrubbed at hard, but without very much success.

'My name's Green. What's yours?'

'Gerda.'

'Gerda what?'

'Does it really matter?' she said patiently, but with a weary air.

'No,' he said heavily. 'No, I don't suppose it does.'

A Guardsman got up from the table across the way and asked him for a light. Green thought it was a bit thick, but he gave the man the light. He turned to the girl and pointed to the divisional sign on the Guardsman's shoulder.

'You see that sign?'

The girl nodded.

'Well, in the Guards they say the eye on it winks when it sees a virgin, and it hasn't winked yet except for one of their own colonels.'

She yawned vaguely and said nothing. He poured another drink.

'Shall we drink brothership?' she asked.

'Yes.'

He filled the glasses again and they intertwined arms and drank bottoms up. Then they kissed with their arms still interlocked. It left them both cold.

'Thou,' he said.

'Thou,' she said.

She watched an old woman trudge by, bent under the weight of a huge sack of potatoes. The woman's grey face and lack-lustre eyes made her shiver in spite of herself.

'Do you want to sleep with me?' she asked suddenly.

'What do you want for the night?' he said, seemingly not every eager.

'It doesn't matter much, does it?' she said. 'But let's finish this whisky first. I feel like a hundred!'

'Ex,' he said, and tipped the glass up.

'Ex,' she repeated, and did the same.

In the year of the General Strike Green's brother wrote to him from Oxford. His brother wrote that he and 'some of the chaps' were going up to 'Town' to help to keep the place going. 'Better not try for a Schol. to Merton. This year it's full of Jews, Reds and Poets.' Would he like to come down for the 'Vac.' and give them a hand?

He accepted his brother's offer and left college at sixteen, never to go back.

His brother drove a tram and he helped as a conductor. The crowds hung about the

146

streets in cloth caps and mufflers, and booed them. They called the students 'plus-four boys' because of their baggy golf-trousers and tasselled stockings. In the morning, when all the clerks and government officials crowded the trams, Green would shout:

'This tram goes anywhere! No fares and kind treatment! Joy rides to the East End!'

This last one made the well-dressed travellers laugh.

Once, a scruffy, undersized cockney, with the Mons Star and other war medals on his torn jacket, tried to get a pram containing a gramophone on the tram. On the side of the pram was chalked in large white letters: 'I have three medals! I speak three languages! I have three children! But I only want ONE JOB!' When Green told the man that he could not bring the pram on, he got nasty and started swearing. Green at sixteen was a head bigger than the man, and he was not afraid.

'What's that?' he said laughing. 'Another one of your languages!'

The clerks inside laughed. The man put one foot on the platform, but Green rang the bell quickly. The man fell in the gutter. When he got up, his chest and medals were all covered in mud. He began to cry.

Once, he and his brother went down to the docks to see a friend, who was with the Guards down there. The streets in that area were crowded with sullen, threatening dockers, but there were plenty of troops about manning machine-gun posts, and Green and his brother felt safe. They heard the sound of martial music as they approached one of the sheds. The tune was 'The British Grenadiers'. It seemed very odd to them and they went to investigate. Inside, they found a fifty-man Guards band playing military marches to an empty shed.

'Just doing our bit,' the tall, debonair Guards officer said, by way of explanation, swinging his swagger-cane like a golf-club.

As they left, the band started playing 'Rule Britannia'.

After the strike ended, Green did not want to go back to his school, and his father did not have any objections – at that time his father was living with a blonde American chorus-girl twenty years his junior, and did not have much time for his sons. He was given a thousand pound a year allowance, and took a flat with his brother, who had come down that year without taking his finals.

London fascinated him, took hold of him, and whirled him from one party to another. That year he went around muttering to himself – and shouting it aloud when he was drunk – 'The world's mine. The world's my oyster!'

Where everything was 'three o'clock in the

morning', the parties fascinated him. There were midnight parties, where everyone had to appear in their sleeping garments, and that horrible woman came in nothing at all – because, as she said: 'she never wore anything in bed'. There were all white parties, where everyone wore white and they danced in the lounge of somebody's flat, hung with lengths of white satin – and that horrible woman came naked because, as she said: 'there's nothing whiter than the human body, is there?' There were swimming parties, where they drank champagne from midnight to six in the morning from little floating tables in a municipal bathing-pool, and that horrible woman took her clothes off and dived in from the twenty-five board and made a terrible belly-flop. When she came out, her full breasts and stomach were an angry red.

Something always seemed to happen at those parties – even if it were only that horrible woman taking her clothes off. There was the man who always brought his pet peke with him and insisted that it should be fed on fresh sweet fruit. Once he caused a scene when the maid did not sweeten the animal's strawberries enough. And he stood over her until she – red-faced and ham-fisted – had poured a full bowl of sugar over them. There was the woman who always insisted – after she had had the requisite number of cocktails – on going into the street and picking up the first man she met. At various times she had dragged in everything from a policeman to a pimp. Sometimes she used to let them make love to her, especially if they were big men – policemen or Guardsmen.

She had some sort of complex about the virility of the working classes. When one of their own circle tried to make love to her, she would smile charmingly and say:

'That's really too, too nice of you, darling. But please don't strain yourself for my sake – really. We all know that you're a pansy, darling.'

Of course, he and his crowd were just on the fringe of things. They talked glibly enough of Noel, Ned, Tallulah, Gertie, Beverley and the rest, but they were not in their class. Still, they had a good time. For him at eighteen there was a succession of girls: skirts just above the knee, pink silk stockings, flat sacklike dresses with strings of pearls down to the waist. They kissed and they fumbled and they went to bed with one another – and it was just the done thing.

Afterwards they had a cocktail and sang something by Noel:

Parisian Pierrot
Society's hero.
The Lord of a day
The Rue de la Paix
Is under your sway.

When he was nineteen, Green went to live with another man. Not that he felt inclined that way, but one had to have a 'gimmick' (though the word was not then current) of some sort. He painted his nails red when he was in the flat and a neutral colour when he went out. He wore a chain-locket around his neck and a heavy gold bracelet round his wrist. When he went to parties – and he found he was invited to more and more parties because of his supposed kink, probably because it flattered the masculinity of the weak specimens that gave them – he painted his face. Once, when he got very drunk, he changed clothes completely with a girl with bobbed hair in front of the whole crowd. Everybody seemed to be taking their clothes off in public that year.

In 1929 Green's boy friend, Henry, went off to Berlin – 'where the boys are girls and the girls are boys'. A lot of the crowd were going away that year, not just to Monte or to the coast, but further afield – Berlin, Sicily, Vienna. That year they were singing 'Bye, bye Black Bird'.

But still the parties went on. They grew even more hectic, but the atmosphere and the spirit seemed to have vanished. He and the crowd discovered they were something called the 'Lost Generation'. The 'Pink Decade' was in, and the Pinks took over.

Now they drank gin in bed-sitters instead of champagne, and they no longer tore the clothes off each other's backs, because they could no longer afford to buy new ones. The parties went on, but Green no longer enjoyed them as he had done once. He felt somehow that life had cheated him, although he didn't know quite how. At twenty-five he was going to parties with the sole intention of getting slewed on booze somebody else had bought. He had not realized that the party could not go on for ever.

ILKA HARMANN

Ilka had noticed him pass twice before, and now he was walking by her seat for the third time, eyeing her. He was eating a chocolate-bar – the paper rolled halfway down the long thin bar. Hungrily, she fixed her eyes on it; she had not had anything to eat since the day before. He stopped when he saw her looking at him, and after a minute he came and sat down beside her.

'Mah name's George,' he said straight away.

'Ich verstehe nicht,' she said.

He smiled, not in the least worried.

'Me – George,' he said, stabbing at his chest with his forefinger.

'Ach so! Georg,' she said comprehending.

'You name?' he said, pointing a finger.

152

'Mein Name? Ich heisse Ilka. Il-ka,' she said, pronouncing the two syllables separately.

'Ilka,' he repeated the word, emphasizing it in his queer foreign fashion. 'Say, that's a queer name!'

'Please?'

'You fine girl, honey. Ah like blonde girls.'

'Please,' she said again.

He pointed to her hair and said:

'Blonde – gut, eh? Where ah come from there ain't no blonde girls. An' if they wuz they wouldn't be fur the likes of me, I guess. Even if ya fight alongside o' them, it don't make any difference – you can bet your last socktoe buck on that!'

She could not understand a word of what he was saying, yet she could see how bitter his face had become. Then suddenly his mood changed as suddenly as it had come. His eyes lit up and his face broke into a good-humoured grin.

'Aw, don't take any notice of me, honey. Ah'm just a goddam mushmouth. Say – you like chocolate? Choc-o-late?' he repeated the word slowly, his thick lips pressed back, revealing gleaming white teeth.

She understood.

'Ja – please.' She was hesitant, but her hunger forced her on. 'Please – I have chocolate – please.'

He opened his haversack, took out a bar of

Hershey chocolate and gave it to her. She tried to eat it slowly, but hunger overcame her and she ate it so greedily that she nearly choked. He slapped her lightly on the back with a big hand.

She smiled her thanks.

'You – hungry girl,' he said, his big brown eyes suddenly serious. 'Ah knows what that is.'

'Please,' she stuttered, the tears mounting up in her eyes.

'You – hungry,' he said. He opened his mouth, pointed his finger at it and made champing noises.

She understood and nodded her head.

'Ja, ich hab' wirklich hunger. Ich hab' seit gestern nichts gegessen.'

He did not understand the words, but he opened his haversack again, took out a package of sandwiches and gave them to her.

'You eat,' he said, pointing to her mouth.

It was getting dark. She would have to be getting back to the bunker, she told herself, if she were going to get a place for the night. He was still talking away happily – as he had been doing for the last half hour – although she could not understand a word.

'Mah sis, Mabel, is a high-yaller girl – tho' ya wouldn't think so to look at me, would ya? She ain't got no time for us now. Why, she's like a frost-bitten water-melon vine in November when she go...'

She interrupted him. She stabbed a finger at herself.

'I go – now – bunker,' she said, very slowly. 'Schlafengehen.' She cocked her head on one side and tucked her two hands under it. 'Schlafenghen – sleepgo.'

His face lost its broad grin.

'Don't go baby!' he said. 'Please, don't go. Ah ain't got no place to go... Ah'm Awol.'

She raised her shoulders in a gesture of puzzled hopelessness.

'Ich verstehe einfach nichts.' She raised one finger. 'Not – one – word – I understand.'

'Me – deserter,' he tried again. 'Nowhere to go.'

'Ach so!' she said. 'Deserteur – Fahnen-fluech-tiger!' and nodded her head.

He put his arm round her shoulder, and after a minute slowly began to pull her face down to his. Somehow it did not seem to matter now that he was a negro.

They were coming out of the park together. He was chattering away again, and she did not stop him – it pleased her somehow. Now and again he looked at her with the eyes of a grateful animal. They were just about to cross the street, when they were stopped by a M.P. patrol.

A tall private, with a face that looked as if

155

it had been chiselled out of the living stone, pressed the end of his white truncheon in George's chest.

'O.K., buster, hold it!' he said in a drawl. 'Where ya going with the dame?'

George looked scared.

'Ah ain't going anywheres in particular, boss,' he said.

The M.P. dropped his truncheon from George's chest as if to consider this statement, picking his nose with the other hand. He looked Ilka up and down with a cocky eye.

'Where did ya get this?' he jerked his thumb at her.

'Ah don't see what that's got to do with you,' George said quietly.

'Hold ya water, soldier,' the tall M.P. drawled, and turned to his companion, a young tough-looking boy. 'Not bad, eh?' he said. 'Get a load of them legs.'

'Yeah,' the other soldier agreed. 'Nicest bit I've seen in a long time.' He leered at Ilka.

George was annoyed.

'Can we go now?' he said suddenly.

The tall M.P. laughed softly.

'I'll have to think about it,' he said.

His companion laughed too.

'Watcha got there?' He pointed with his white truncheon in the direction of George's haversack.

'Just a few duds,' George said hesitantly.

'Open up.'

'But, ah told ya,' George protested. 'It's just a few o' ma duds...'

'Blow it out!' the tall M.P. snapped, his grin gone. 'Open up – and that's an order, soldier!'

Slowly, George began to unbuckle the straps of his haversack. He opened it and held it out for inspection. The tall M.P. poked his truncheon underneath and forced him to hold it up higher.

'So,' he said. 'Just a few duds, eh?' With his free hand he foraged among the bars of chocolate and the packets of cigarettes that the haversack contained. 'What you aiming to do, nigger boy? Buy yaself half of Jarmany?'

Suddenly, without warning, he brought his foot up under the haversack and sent it flying out of George's hands – its contents cascading out on to the pavement.

After a moment, George bent down and began to pick up the packets of cigarettes. The tall M.P. winked at his companion and raised his boot to kick George. Ilka saw what he was about to do and shouted:

'Georg!'

Then she ran at the M.P. He ducked as she grabbed at him, and with a sneer, pushed her against the railings.

'Keep out of this, you Heinie bitch!' he hissed.

George got to his feet quickly. His hand slid down to his hip-pocket and brought out a pocket-knife. With a sliding movement of his thumbnail he pressed the long, narrow blade of the knife out.

'All right, boss,' he said very quietly. 'If that's the way ya want it.'

The young M.P.'s hand went down to his automatic, but the tall one shook his head.

'No,' he said, his cold eyes fixed on the knife in George's hand. 'I'll deal with this chicken nigger...'

And at that moment he threw his truncheon, with a grunt, at George. It caught him squarely in the face, and he went down with a faint groan, the knife clattering out of his hand on to the pavement.

Then the two M.P.s were upon him, pounding at him with their feet and clubs. George held his hands clenched over his head, but they started kicking him in the ribs and stomach, and he had to lower them again to protect these parts. The tall M.P. kicked him savagely on the temple, and he became unconscious.

The two M.P.s stood there over the motionless body, panting, with clenched fists. Ilka ran forward, but the younger of the two caught her by the hair. For a moment he held her there, with her hair twined in his big fingers.

'O.K., sister,' he said. 'Beat it!' and gave

158

her a push away from him.

She stood there, looking at him through tear-clouded eyes. He fixed her with his cold eyes.

'Sister, I said beat it … an' that's what I mean! On your way!' He paused for a moment, and looked down at George. He laughed. 'You won't be seeing this character for a long time, anyway – baby.'

At that moment a police jeep drew up at the kerb, and the two M.P.s began to drag George by the arms across the pavement to it. With a grunt and a heave they lifted him into the back of the jeep. Then they drove off. Ilka watched them go. She was crying.

In order to buy a piece of clothing in Germany that summer, one needed a 'Bezugschein' – a permit – and even if one managed to obtain a 'Bezugschein', there was probably not a shop in town which would be able to supply the cloth for it.

She had taken her winter coat for repair some six weeks before, and now she was calling at the tailor's for the third time to ask if her coat were ready. The fat woman behind the counter looked at her in such a way as to make her feel shabbier and thinner than she really was.

'Yes,' the woman said lazily. 'What do you want?'

'I've come about my coat,' she said

timidly, and laid the ticket on the counter.

The fat woman felt tired after the party of the night before, but she made a pretence of searching for the coat. She thumbed her way through the shabby grey and black coats hanging in the back of the shop for a minute, and then sat down heavily on her chair at the counter.

''Fraid I can't find it,' she said with a sigh.

'What do you mean – you can't find it?' the woman asked anxiously. 'I've been here twice already, and both times you've told me that it would be ready soon! Please let me have my coat!'

'I tell you, I can't find it,' the fat woman said patiently.

'You mean it's – lost!' the woman said, panic-stricken.

'I'm afraid so,' the woman said calmly, having experienced many such scenes in the last few months.

'But what am I going to do? I must have a coat for the winter months – I'll freeze to death if I don't. I live in a ruin with no... You must get me a coat. You must!' She almost spat the words into the fat woman's face. 'You're responsible for it.'

The fat woman breathed out deeply – her corsets were sticking into her. The next time they were expecting a scene like this, she told herself, she'd get her husband to deal with it. She didn't see why he should sit on

160

his fat backside all day long reading thrillers, whilst she did all the hard graft.

'If you look at the back of the ticket,' she said, 'you'll see that the management does not hold itself responsible for the return of articles brought for repair, but that it does undertake to refund the cost price of any article lost. I don't think we can do fairer than that, do you?'

Christ, she thought, I'm getting to know the words off by heart like a poem or something.

The woman raised her head from reading the back of the ticket.

'Tell me the price,' the fat woman said, 'and I'll gladly refund the full amount.'

'But,' the woman protested, 'you know full well I can't buy a coat anywhere. Oh, what am I going to do this winter?'

The fat woman shrugged her shoulders.

'I don't know anything about that,' she said. For a moment she felt a kind of pity for the woman. With that figure of hers no man would give her a second look – so she wouldn't be able to earn herself a coat that way. 'If you go down to the Bezugschein people in a couple of months' time when it starts getting cold and...'

She stopped speaking. The woman was crying softly to herself. She lost patience.

'All right,' she snapped. 'Turn off the flood. How much do you want for your damned coat? I haven't got all day, you know…'

But the woman did not answer. Slowly she turned, with the bit of rag she used for a handkerchief held up to her nose, and walked out of the shop. The doorbell tinkled stupidly, and she was gone.

The fat woman stared after her for a moment in surprise, scratching her stomach the whole time. Then she got up from her chair and slouched in her carpet slippers into the back room, where her husband lay on the couch reading and smoking a Camel. He was good-looking in a soft, blond way, and was twenty years younger than she was. A refugee from the Russian Zone, he had married her to get a roof over his head and something to fill his belly. There were a lot of these so-called 'fried potato relationships' that summer.

'Ooh, you are a lazy sow,' she said, breathing with difficulty because of her corsets.

'What's the matter, Mammy?' he asked, without looking up from his thriller.

'I go working my fingers to the bone, sitting up all night altering those damned coats, and then have to sit all day in the shop listening to those miseries complain. I've had a nose-full, I can tell you!'

'Don't be angry with me, Mammy,' he said softly. 'You know that since I was wounded I can't do a thing.'

Her mood changing suddenly, she went

across and stroked his long, carefully waved, blond hair lovingly. Then she bent down and kissed his forehead, like she'd seen them do in the cinema.

Oh, my face, he thought, how she does smell.

Dutifully, he put his arm around her.

'Do you know, Schnuggi?' she said, as he drew her down. 'We'll make four or five hundred on that last coat. It wasn't bad stuff, and that little woman round...'

'Don't talk business now, Mammy,' he said thickly, trying to simulate passion. Oh, my face, he thought, how she does stink!

In July, Black Market prices remained fairly constant:
Bread – 56-60 Marks.
White Bread – 40 Marks (stolen, of course, from the army).
Butter – 250 Marks.
Coffee – 600 Marks (slightly more for beans than for tinned coffee).
Sugar – not noted.
Potatoes – 100-110 Marks per hundred-weight.
Cigarettes – English and American – 5 Marks each.
Price constant in the Zones. Slightly higher in Berlin.

'I went with me bit of frat to the tailor's to

get a civvy suit made. I'd just come out of dock, and I thought like it would be better to get a steady bit. Sort of get me feet under the table. So I thought it would be better to get a civvy suit – easier for getting around like. Little bent-up feller fixed me up with one in blue pin-stripe stuff for thirteen hundred fags. Said one of me shoulders were higher than t'other and he was gonna pad one side like. I thought it was a bit of a cheek from Jerry. He was no beauty, either. So when I got me suit I gave him a thousand. What could he do about it? Me bit of frat started nattering about knowing the bloke well and all that cock, but I soon told her where to get off. I stopped her fags and she soon came round. Do anything for fags the Jerries will…'

Strange prison. They made him walk along a corridor, which was traversed by another corridor. When he reached the place where they crossed, shots were fired in front of him. They put him in a cell like a shower-bath. It was filled up with water from a pipe in the roof and he had to pump the water out with a handle in order to save himself from drowning. Queer people, though. One of the guards, who used to beat him up now and again, came into his cell every evening and played a kind of football in the narrow space. Football mad, some of them.

JIMMIE

It was on Company Orders that afternoon. The whole of the company was going – even the cooks. Personal weapons were to be taken and mortars and Brens were to be drawn from the armourer's. It was the talk of the cookhouse that evening.

'Hey! What's this lark we're on tomorrow?'

'Escort duty, can't you read, Jack!'

'But I mean to say. Why all the shocking armaments? We're taking Brens and the bloody lot. T'ord bondhook ought ter be enough. It's only escort duty, after all.'

Another voice:

'Haven't yer heard? We're gonna escort a thousand S.S. men – all over six foot three and as dangerous as ah don't know what!'

'Go on!'

'Honest; I heard it from a bloke in the Q.M.'s who heard it...'

They took their places in the trucks – one at the front with the driver and one at the back with the tightly packed-in prisoners. Jimmie lost the toss and Charlie, who had just come back from hospital, went in front. The thousand S.S. men turned out to be three hundred civilian internees who had been rounded up in the district for suspected affiliation to the Nazi Party. Now they shuffled forward – mostly old men –

and let themselves be jammed thirty in a truck as if it happened every day of their lives. The convoy leader moved slowly round the cobbled courtyard and through the gate. The rest of the trucks started to follow. Outside, the street was lined with women and children – presumably relatives – who had somehow got wind of the move. As the trucks slowed down at the gate, several women tried to hand packages to the men, but a M.P. officer knocked them out of their hands with his cane on to the road, where they were squashed by the wheels of the next truck. Here and there a woman would recognize a relative and start to shout and wave, but for the most part the women stood there in silence; black, bowed figures pinching their handkerchiefs to their noses.

Jimmie sat on the tailboard with his rifle gripped between his knees. He was glad that they were finally out of town. He lit a cigarette with difficulty, and then became aware of thirty pairs of eyes fixed upon him. He could not smoke with them all watching him, and after a moment he stubbed the cigarette out, blew on the end and put it back in the packet. A moment later, he took the packet out again and handed it to the man next to him.

'There's only fifteen,' he said slowly in German. 'You'll have to break them in two.'

In case the man had not understood, he

took one cigarette out of the packet and broke it in two halves.

Eventually, they got the cigarettes passed round and everyone was smoking. Jimmie was a little afraid that somebody might pass and see them smoking, but they had all finished before the major went by in his jeep.

'You ought to save the ends,' he told the man standing next to him.

The man smiled, and said he would.

'You speak good German,' he said nervously. 'You learnt it at school?'

Jimmie laughed.

'No, they didn't teach German at my school. I've been in Germany nine months now and learnt what I know here.'

'What are you doing here?' he asked the man. The man seemed eager to explain his case.

'I'm professor of history,' he said. 'I had nothing to do with the Party. One day last...'

A professor of history – an educated man, Jimmie thought, and he tells me that I can speak good German, although I can hardly string three words together. It's sickening the way some of these Jerries flatter you.

'What kind of a professor were you?' he asked the man, who had just finished speaking. 'Perhaps that's why they put you in...' he did not know the word for 'prison', so he left the sentence unfinished.

167

'Ich war Professor der Chinesischen Geschichte,' he replied. Chinese history, Jimmie translated to himself. That doesn't seem to have much to do with politics.

Two hours later they arrived at their destination. With a grinding of gears the trucks turned off the main road down into a sort of a gully in which the internment camp was situated. Jimmie's backside was sore from sitting on the iron tailboard and, giving his rifle to the professor, he dropped over the side of the truck and went nearly up to his ankles in mud. The place was a sea of mud for all it was mid-July. Jimmie supposed it was because the place was in the middle of the gully.

Charlie got out of the front of the truck stiffly.

'That trip didn't do my cold any good,' he said thickly, and Jimmie laughed. 'It's dribbling again.'

The professor handed down his rifle, and they plodded heavily through the mud to the grass verge.

They looked at the camp. It was the typical German P.O.W. camp: a square of double-aproned barbed wire with a watch-tower at each corner of the square. Inside there was no sign of life. A union jack hung lifelessly from the top of a freshly whitewashed pole in the centre of the square.

Suddenly, a whistle blew and a group of

elderly men ran out of one of the huts as if the devil himself were after them. They were followed out by a Jewish-looking corporal. He gave a sharp order in German, and the men formed up in a double line in front of him as if they were soldiers.

'Number off!' he shouted in German. The men numbered off smartly, but they weren't fast enough for him. He bellowed at them for a long minute in fluent German, which was too fast for Jimmie to follow. Then he gave the order 'left turn!' and chased them round the patch of green for five minutes.

He halted them, and smiled balefully.

'Right!' he said in English, for the benefit of his audience. 'Yer like a lot of pregnant penguins! We're gonna smart that drill up if it takes us all day. Get that? If it takes all day!'

His voice rose to a crescendo on the last word in the approved drill-sergeant manner. The men standing to attention did not presumably understand his words, but they saw from his manner what he meant. Jimmie could see that one of the men in the front rank, with a red face and white hair, looked as if he were about to cry.

'About turn!' the corporal bellowed in German. 'By the left – double march!'

The men now started running across a stretch of open ground some hundred yards in length, which was just a sea of liquid mud. Most of the men wore wooden heel-less slippers, which remained stuck in the mud, but they ran on without them in their bare feet.

The corporal remained at the edge of the mud and shouted his orders, which were simply 'HINLEGEN! – get down!' Where-upon everybody flopped straight down on their faces in the mud 'AUFSTEHEN! – get up!' and 'KEHRT LINKS UM! – left turn!' The men ran – flopped down – got up and struggled on. This continued for ten minutes before the corporal brought them to a halt on the firm ground.

He let them rest for a moment – their chests heaving, threatening to burst – and then bellowed 'STILL-GESTANDEN!' – attention!' The men stiffened into the wooden German position of attention: feet out like ducks, elbow slightly bent and away from the body, the tips of the fingers just touching the cloth of the trousers. The cor-poral looked at his handiwork for a moment, and then, after knocking the mud off his boots on the stone steps of the hut, he went inside, leaving them standing there.

A black stain started to grow on the pants of one of the men.

'Look at him,' somebody shouted. 'He's done it in his pants!'

Perhaps the man had expected a laugh, but nobody did so. There was movement in the camp now. A sergeant-major appeared from the hut nearest the gate, followed by several soldiers with pick-axe handles held in their hands. Behind them came a corporal, who for no apparent reason was wearing a steel helmet and carrying a sten-gun.

The sergeant-major, a florid man well over six foot with a little moustache, saw them watching the Germans standing to attention, and smiled.

'We always do that by way of reception,' he said. 'Frightens the living daylights out of the Jerries.'

The sergeant-major found the major and, after the usual formalities had been gone through, the prisoners started to get out of the trucks and line up in the mud. The sergeant-major gave an order, and the first truckload moved through the gate in double file. As they did so, the soldiers prodded them in the ribs with their pick-handles and knocked the carved sticks that some of the older men carried into the mud. One of the prisoners started to argue, but a kick in the backside sent him flying into the mud.

The next truck-load started going through. Up above, on the road, a ramshackle three-wheel van stopped and a boy got out and walked to the verge, presumably to relieve himself.

The corporal in the steel helmet saw this, and raised his arm – Jimmie noticed that his

171

sleeve bore three golden wound stripes –
and pointed to one of the many notices that
lined that stretch of the road: 'No stopping.
Minimum speed – 10 m.p.h.'

'Can't you bloody shocking Germans
read?' he screamed.

The boy looked around him puzzled,
wondering what the corporal meant. He
shrugged his shoulders, and was about to
proceed with what he had intended when
the corporal raised his sten to his shoulder
and fired. The burst crackled in the leaves of
the tree about the boy's head. He made a
spectacular dive for cover, and a moment
later the van disappeared down the road in
a cloud of dust.

'Damn me! Did you see that?' Charlie
asked. 'That bloke must be off his rocker.
He could have easily killed that kid – yer
know what sten-guns are. Fancy shooting at
a kid because he wanted a leak!' He lowered
his tone confidentially, and gave Jimmie a
dig in the ribs. 'If you ask me, the Gestapo
had nowt on these lads. There's no flies on
them. Look over there!'

Jimmy's eyes followed the direction of
Charlie's gaze – past the group of men still
standing rigidly to attention – to the solitary
figure running up and down the main square.
From the way he held himself, Jimmie could
see that he was an old man. The man held a
bucket in each hand filled with something

heavy – perhaps sand or water – and he was being doubled from one end of the square to the other by a soldier with a stick in his hand. When he got to one end of the square, the soldier would shout 'double mark time!' and then walk over slowly until he reached the man. If he was not bringing his knees up high enough, the soldier would tap him repeatedly across them until he did so. When he got weary of this, the performance would begin again, and the man would be sent off running for the other end of the square.

Now, the whole company was stretched out along the barbed-wire fence, looking at the man. Some of them began to mutter under their breath. Somebody said:

'What's 'e doing to yon poor sod?'

Somebody else said:

'What is this place, anyway?'

The sergeant-major, who had been busy at the gate, came across and said:

'Don't feel sorry for the bugger, lads…'

'Have you noticed how they always call us "lads" when they want something out of us?' Jimmie whispered to Charlie quickly.

'He's a real Nazi that one. Why…'

'Ay, like the one in my truck,' a voice interrupted the sergeant-major. 'He'd only come to Germany last month from Jugoslavia. First time he'd ever seen the place – an' he were supposed to be a Nazi!'

'Ar,' another voice said in agreement. 'Like

the one I had. A couple of Yanks stopped him in the street and tore his papers up. Said they'd lost a prisoner and were taking him in his place…'

'This bloke's a real War Criminal,' the sergeant-major bellowed above the row, his face red. 'He was a professor…'

'Don't give us that bull!' a half-dozen voices shouted.

'Oh, you lads can't know about these things!' the sergeant-major bellowed back.

'Oh, can't we – can't we?' the crowd jeered. 'We bloody well can't…'

At that moment Major Telford, attracted by the shouting, walked over from his jeep.

'All right!' he snapped, holding his hand above his head for silence. 'That's enough of that. You're like a lot of silly washer-women! The S.M.'s right. These men are War Criminals – and they deserve to suffer for it. Don't you puzzle your brains about the rights and wrongs of it. Somebody more competent than yourselves has already decided that. All that you've got to do is to obey your orders!'

He paused, and looked at them for a moment, making them feel like a bunch of schoolboys caught out by the headmaster. It's queer, Jimmie thought, how an officer can get away with it. Probably any one of these blokes here could knock the stuffing out of the officer – yet he has them just where he wants them.

'Right, sergeant major,' the major said, turning to the W.O. 'They're all yours now.'

The sergeant-major saluted smartly. 'Thank you, sir,' he said, and gave a look at the men over the officer's shoulder. The major gave an order, and the soldiers began to file back to their trucks. They went quietly, with here and there a man mumbling under his breath.

It began to rain, and Jimmie plodded his way through the mud as quickly as he could. He got into the truck. He looked out of the back and saw the sergeant-major snap his fingers in the air. The corporal in the steel helmet dashed away quickly into the hut near the gate. A few minutes later he reappeared, carrying a white officer-type raincoat. Carefully – almost reverently – he laid it around the sergeant-major's shoulders. The sergeant-major gave no sign that he had noticed the corporal, and went on looking at the prisoners shuffling through the gate.

Christ, Jimmie thought. I wonder what goes on in this place.

'Hey, gie's a leg-up,' Charlie shouted. 'I'm going to come in the back with you. That feller in the front gets on my wick with his moaning.'

Jimmie reached down and gave Charlie a hand up.

'Phew,' Charlie said, wiping the rain off his forehead with the back of his hand. 'My cold's giving me jip. It's dribbling like hell.'

'Is that bad?' Jimmie asked. Charlie shrugged his shoulders.

'You could shock me,' he said. 'I wouldn't know.'

They looked at the prison camp again.

'It's funny really,' Jimmie said, 'but if Jerry won another war we'd be regarded as War Criminals.'

'How do you make that out?' Charlie asked, interested.

'Well, this place isn't exactly a home from home,' Jimmie said.

'Too bloody Irish, it ain't,' Charlie agreed heartily. 'I've been in Nicks which were luxury hotels agen this place. It gives me the willies just to look at it.'

'Well, we've helped to put people in it, so, technically, I suppose we're just as guilty as the ordinary S.S. man was.'

'Christ,' Charlie said. 'I've never thought of it like that before.'

'Well, do that little thing,' Jimmie said, with a half-grin. 'And afterwards give three cheers for democracy for me, will you?'

They sat in silence for a minute or two. Then Charlie spoke:

'Have a Wood,' he said, and offered Jimmie a cigarette from a paper packet.

'Thanks, Charlie,' Jimmie said, and

accepted it. 'You're not a bad old devil, are you?'

As they left, the group of men still stood to attention on the patch of green, but now they rocked like young trees in the wind, and on the square the man with the two buckets was still stumbling up and down to the command of the soldier with the stick in his hand.

CHAPTER V

AUGUST

And Abraham drew near and said: Wilt thou
also destroy the righteous with the wicked?
Peradventure there be fifty righteous within
the city.

Hamburger Echo. 1.8.45
22 people died in the streets of the city last
month: the deaths were attributed to
hunger. In the same period 15 murders and
11,000 cases of breaking and entering were
reported in Greater Hamburg.

Die Welt. 5.8.45
The Frauenterror was apprehended late last
night in the Dammtor area. He was the
D.P., Olle K. The Frauenterror used to wait
in the ruins of one of the more isolated parts
of the city and rob and strip unsuspecting
women. The garments he acquired this way
were later sold on the Black Market.

Hamburger Abendblatt. 10.8.45
180 new cases of active T.B. reported last week in the city against a weekly average of 30 pre-war.

Die Woche. 13.8.45
...motor police patrols managed to apprehend one of the youthful thieves. He was Rudolf Z., aged 16. He said that after the iron fencing had been erected on either side of the railway line to stop the plundering of the coal trucks, his gang hit upon the idea of holding an iron bar over the top of the line and in this way knock off the coal. He told our reporter...

D.P.D. 15.8.45
It was reported today that more than five times as many old people are dying monthly in Hamburg than before the war. Since the beginning of the month, more than 30 old people have died in the city. This compares with the figures of 25 for the month of July.

Die Welt. 19.5.45
Professor Dr. —, the City's Public Health Director, was today received by the representatives of the British Occupation Power. The ever-increasing V.D. figures were dis-

cussed. The professor said later that he had been told there had been nearly 25,000 cases of V.D. among British troops in the last two months. A campaign of public enlightenment will be launched in the city next month. The professor told reporters that they had had cases of girls of thirteen…

D.P.D. 20.5.45
The district of Billstedt (pop. 260,000) announced its list of 'Bezugscheine' for the month of July. There were permits for 56 Cardigans, 49 Frocks, 4 Babies' Napkins, 3 Rubber Sheets, 7 kilos of Knitting Wool and 21 small Bath Towels. During the same period there were 183 births.

Hamburger Echo. 24.5.45
The British Occupation Power intends to erect a large club for its troops in the centre of the city during the coming months. The 'Victory Club', as it will be called, will cost 13 million marks, which will come from reparations. The work comprises dining-rooms, shops, ball-rooms, reading-rooms, bath-rooms, play-rooms…

Suicide. Girl left note. 'No coat for winter.' Four blind from drinking Black Market schnapps. Manager of St Pauli café accused.

Standard sleeping space regulations altered.
10 square metres minimum requirement.

Officer says: 'Germans no initiative.'

...reliably reported from refugees who ...
across the frontier 'black' ... large scale
deportations of German nationals ...
Russian Occupation Power...

THE SERGEANT

They had been walking for days now, and
the blind man had not complained once.
Nearly a week before they had fought their
way on to a train and had hung on for dear
life to one of the buffers, but after travelling
for some hours the train had stopped
because it had run out of fuel. Since then
they had been walking. Yesterday they had
eaten the last of their food, but still the blind
man did not complain. Now they were well
within the frontier area, and, as they
threaded their way through the thick pine
forest, they talked in whispers – just in case.

'You're sure that your mother is going to
want me?' the sergeant asked, as he had
asked many times in the last few weeks.

The blind man smiled in his queer lop-
sided way.

'Of course. You'll be the only able-bodied

man in the place. You can't see me spreading muck, can you?'

'Do you really use human muck?' the sergeant asked, happy now at the assurance.

'Yes,' the blind man said. 'Every week or so the farmers send their carts into the village, and then they suck it out of the privies with this long tube I told you about...'

At that moment they heard distant rifle fire, and they fell silent. For a moment they halted, and then they went on, but without speaking.

As they walked on, the sergeant thought back over the last few weeks with the blind man. A month ago he could not have cared whether he died or not – perhaps on the road he had wanted to die – but now he wanted to live. After he had been wounded in the shoulder that day, they had hidden in the forest until he had recovered enough to go on. The blind man had tended his wound the best he could. He had doped the sergeant with sleeping tablets from his bundle, and then squeezed the bullet out of his shoulder. He had gone back into the town and begged food from the Russian kitchens – they had not harmed him because he was blind. The blind man had set traps for the rabbits and the badgers and they ate the meat, made soap from the fat, with the aid of soapstone and pine needles, for his wound and exchanged the pelts for food.

In the days they spent together in the forest, they talked and talked about nearly everything under the sun. And one night the blind man had confessed that he was not alone in the world, but that he had a mother, who lived on a little farm in Westphalia, but he was afraid to go home because of his blindness.

'What good would a blind man be on a farm?'

The sergeant, who had once hated all men, began to talk and try to persuade the blind man to go home. And when the blind man was persuaded, he wanted the sergeant to go with him. And, as they lay in the long grass under the purple night of the hot summer sky, he would tell the sergeant of his home and its people.

'And in November we have the "Schlacht-fest" – the "killing-feast" when we kill the pigs. They kill a pig and slit its throat. And the women fill the bowls with the blood from its throat and stir with their hands – the blood red up to their elbows – before it stiffens for the blood sausage. And then they scrape the skin clean of hairs and begin to hack the carcass up. And at night the neighbours come and eat fried chops and drink Schlichte...

'When the farmers make a sale in the market on a Saturday, they spit on their palms and slap them together hard as a sign of their agreement...

'And when the girl is married, they make her dance with her husband in the room and everybody rushes and tugs at her veil to tear a piece off which will bring good luck and...

'And this poacher used to push the pram through the woods with his wife on his arm. And the foresters used to say: "Why don't you ever come shooting these days, Herr Schmitz?" But he used to shake his head and say he was too old for that sort of thing. And when they were out of sight, he would take his rifle out from beneath the baby in the pram and hunt the wild pig...'

Gradually, the sergeant built himself a picture of the life in the remote village in the Westphalian forest, and the desire to go there grew in him. One night he said simply to the blind man:

'When I am better I would like to go with you – home.'

The blind man was overjoyed, and it was decided there and then. And every day they waited with growing impatience for his wound to heal sufficiently for them to go on.

The sergeant was jerked out of his day-dreaming by the sight of the river, which they had to cross, in front of them. They sat down on the bank and waited until it was dark. They shared the sergeant's last cigarette end, and stared across the river to the British Zone on the other side.

About nine, they stripped and tied their clothes around their boots, which they fixed on their heads by string. The sergeant helped the blind man with his. Over to the right a searchlight was suddenly switched on, and a moment later they heard the rattle of small-arms fire. Then all was silent again. The sergeant gripped the blind man's arm tightly.

'Listen' he whispered. 'You go into the river here and I'll go in a little lower down – just in case...' He did not complete the sentence.

'I'm not afraid,' the blind man said. 'I trust you – comrade.'

The sergeant grinned, forgetting that his companion could not see his grin.

The water was surprisingly cold after the heat of the day. It struck the sergeant in the belly with a shock that made him feel like urinating. He looked to his right and saw that the blind man was in the water too, waiting for him to give the O.K.

'All right,' he said. 'Let's go – now!'

The blind man struck out with a powerful breast stroke, and he followed a moment later with a side stroke so that he could keep an eye on him.

The river current seemed more powerful than he had anticipated, and he looked anxiously in the direction of the blind man, but he was still moving forward at a steady stroke. He was quite warm now. Suddenly in the distance he heard shouting. God, he thought, this is it, and waited for the stream of tracer to come pricking the water with its iron fingers. But none came. Then he realized why – the shouting was coming from the British side of the river. He trod water for a moment, and looked. On the other side he could make out eight or nine figures in battle-dress waiting for them. He had some difficulty getting the blind man up the muddy, slippy bank, but one of the soldiers came down and gave him a hand. They dressed whilst the soldiers stood there, rifles in hand, watching them. Afterwards, somebody pushed a cigarette in his hand and said:

'Here yer are, mate. Yer must be frozo. It's real parky, ternight!'

He lit up and gave the blind man a draw.

'Shock me drunk!' another soldier said to the one who had given them the cigarette. 'What's the matter with you, whacker? Think yer are the bloody Red Cross?'

'Aw, stuff you, Nobby!' the soldier replied. 'We ain't all greedy guts like you. Can't yer see the bleeders is frozen?'

It was when the patrol started to lead the way down the path along the bank of the river that the sergeant realized that they were Guardsmen. It was the way that they formed up and marched off across the rough country that gave them away. He had another surprise when they were marched into the hut which formed the control point at the end of the Bailey bridge which linked the Russians and the British. The officer in charge was the lieutenant of two years before in Italy – only now he was a captain. The sergeant was scared, but the light in the hut was bad and he had changed a lot since two years before in Italy. He kept his head down – as a man who had just swum a powerful river might.

The officer drawled out his questions in the same languid tone as two years before in Italy.

'Who are you? Where have you come from? Who's the blind man? Did you see any Russian troops on the other side? Were they armoured or just infantry? Did he notice any...'

The sergeant kept his head lowered and mumbled to every question:

'Nix versteh'. Nix versteh'.'

'Could I help, sir?' the Dutch interpreter-sergeant, standing behind the officer, interrupted, but the officer waved him away.

'I'll deal with this,' he said. 'All these people understand English. They only pretend they don't when it suits their purpose. It was just the same with the wogs in Italy.'

He pointed to the blind man, sitting on a box near the door.

'Come here, you,' he said.

The blind man did not move, but the corporal standing behind him took his arm and propelled him forward gently.

'You – Nazi?' the officer barked. The blind man, not knowing that he was being addressed, did not reply.

This did not seem to discourage the officer, and he said:

'Where were you wounded? In Russia? Do you like the Russians?'

The blind man was silent.

'Oh, God, what a stupid fool,' the sergeant thought. 'What a stupid fool.'

The captain stroked the weedy moustache that he did not have two years before. In the Guards it was not done to grow a moustache until one was at least a captain. After some moments' silence he turned to the corporal.

'Turn them back to the Russkies,' he said.

The corporal moved forward to carry out the order, but the sergeant held up his hand and spoke.

'Please, sir,' he tried to disguise his English. 'Do not send us back to the Russians.'

The officer smiled up at the interpreter.

'I told yer so, Klaas,' he said. 'They all speak English. Why shouldn't I send you back?'

The sergeant almost said, 'Permission to speak, sir?', but he restrained himself in time.

'If we … er … go back the Russians will put us … er … in prison.'

The officer remained silent for a moment, and then said:

'Have you forgotten something – sir! When you speak to a British officer you say "sir" – get that!'

'I am sorry – sir,' the sergeant mumbled. 'But can we stay, sir?'

The officer shook his head.

'No can do. Too many of you already. No food for the lot of you.'

The sergeant dropped his accent.

'Then let the blind man stay, at least,' he said.

The officer looked up at him with interest.

'You suddenly speak remarkably good English,' he said. They looked at each other hard for a moment in the yellow light of the oil lamp, and then the officer lost interest. He waved his hand in a gesture of dismissal.

'All right, Corporal,' he said. 'Take them over the bridge to our dearly beloved Allies. Victors of Stalingrad, Conquerors of Berlin, and all that bull.'

'Hard luck,' the corporal, who was a communist from Greenock, whispered to them as he led them away.

The Russians took away their braces and

189

the blind man's watch, then put them in a camp in the middle of the wood. It was full of men, women and children who had been caught trying to cross the frontier 'black' like themselves and were now awaiting the Russians' pleasure. For the men, the Russians' pleasure meant a blow on the side of the head with a rifle-butt when they got drunk. For the women, it meant a nightly visit and rape in one of the sheds. Old women – over sixty – were specially favoured like this because they were at that age supposed to be free from disease and to bring luck to soldiers in battle.

In the middle of the night, some seven days after they had been brought there, a whole party of them were marched to the nearest railway station. Here they were lined up along the platform, and Russian officers in long grey coats and stiff peaked caps began to move down the line, stopping now and again to examine the physique of some particular man or woman. If the persons were not satisfactory, they were sent across the platform to join the group of children, who had already been separated from their parents. It was then that the people realized what was going on. A murmur of protest ran down the ranks. A woman began to cry. The Russian guards levelled their automatics. And all the time the blind man tugged the sergeant's sleeve and asked:

'What's going on? What's going on?'

But the sergeant remained silent. The Russian gave the blind man's pitted face a quick glance, but did not stop.

The senior Russian officer gave an order, and the young boys in cloth blouses and side hats moved forward slowly, forcing the crowd back against the waiting cattle-trucks. The blind man became aware of the muttering and movement around him and felt for the sergeant's hand, but at the moment a sudden motion of the crowd forced the sergeant away from him. He sought desperately for the hand. People began to scream and shout. He shouted the sergeant's name aloud. Somebody gave him a push, and he fell over a bundle that had been dropped on the platform.

'Comrade,' he shouted. 'Where are you!' And somebody put a foot on his back and knocked all the wind out of him.

The sergeant fought desperately against the crowd to get back to the place where he had seen the blind man fall. He clawed savagely and recklessly at the people pressed tight against him in terror of the Russians.

'Get out of my way – you bastard!' he screamed in English, and punched the stupid lost face of an old man in front of him. A woman lifted her two hands to protect herself from him, but he pushed her violently to one side. But it was no good. It was like fighting against a strong current. Gradually – and almost imperceptibly – he was forced back towards the cattle-trucks. His arms were pressed tightly against his sides and he felt himself sinking. It was as if he were drowning. His strength drained from him, and he could fight no longer.

The naked bulbs of the station glared down upon an empty platform. The train gave a grunt and covered it for a moment with a cloud of grey steam. Then it was gone. The blind man lay flat on his face among the pathetic litter that the people had left behind them. The little red light of the end coach of the train was still visible in the distance, but the blind man was dead.

GREEN

Green and the girl, Gerda, sat on the Terrasse overlooking the estuary, drinking Rhine wine. They had been living together for three weeks now.

'Have another glass of wine,' he said, seeing her glass was empty.

She took the bottle out of the bucket, but it was empty. Green clicked his fingers for the waiter.

'Ober, could we have another bottle of wine?' he said.

The waiter smiled, as he knew Green well now.

'I'll see what I can do, sir,' he said.

He came back with another bottle of the same wine and put it in the bucket.

'190 marks, sir,' he said.

'Five marks per cigarette – that's approximately forty cigarettes,' Green reckoned aloud.

'I'm sorry, sir,' the waiter said, 'but we've to hand in marks at the cash desk.'

Green said nothing, but took a fifty tin of cigarettes out of his pocket.

'Here's fifty,' he said. 'See if you can sell that and pay the bill. The other ten's for you.'

'Thank you, sir. I'll do that straight away.'

It was an old trick, Green knew, but he didn't mind.

'By the way,' he said. 'What's happened to the orchestra? Why isn't it playing?'

'We're having a cabaret, sir,' the waiter said. 'Starts in about ten minutes' time.'

Green nodded his head and poured out two glasses of wine.

'It's a "spritziger",' he said. 'I prefer it to the other.'

The girl said nothing.

'Do you know "Faust"?' he said, after a moment's silence.

'Oh, yes,' she said. 'We did Goethe at school.' She thought hard for a moment. '"Through this narrow street, he must come",' she quoted. 'We always used to quote that when we were waiting for boys after school. A kind of joke, you know. How silly we must have been.'

'That's Schiller,' he said.

'Oh.'

'Do you know? – "For man must quail at bridges never crossed. Lamenting even things he never lost".'

'No. Is it "Faust"?'

'Yes.'

'Why do you quote it to me?'

'Well … I can't explain it very well. It's like reading a very long novel – "War and … Peace". Is that the correct German title?'

'I suppose so.'

'You read something like that. It bores you, but still, when you put it down, finished – it's as if something important's gone out of your life. Well, it's like that with me. Here I am in my thirties and…'

Inside, the music started to play, and the girl, who was bored, interrupted him.

'Shall we go and have a look?' she said. 'I haven't seen a show since March.'

'O.K.,' he said, and they rose, carrying their glasses in with them.

The place was full of soldiers seated in a circle round the dance-floor at small tables, drinking weak German beer. The lights dimmed and the cabaret began. The first act was a juggler with cups. Green was bored, but the soldiers were delighted and cheered wildly. The next act consisted of two female trapeze artistes. At the end of the act, one of the big blondes came down the rope, hands first. Suddenly, her left breast flopped out. When she reached the floor she smoothed her hair and then put her breast back in her decorated brassière. The soldiers cheered and whistled wildly and began to rain cigarettes on the dance-floor as a sign of their approval. The woman had been losing her breast every night for the last five years since it first happened by accident. The audiences liked it.

'It's like when a woman gets out of a car,' Green said to the girl. 'A man sees up her skirt and gets a thrill. They can see pictures of naked women any time, but that is something accidental, secret, that exists between them and the woman. They get a kick from it.'

Green was bored and, leaving the girl, he went back to the table. In the corner of the deserted Terrasse a thin black dog was sitting on the pebbles looking at him mournfully. Something about the dog made him afraid. He shivered and searched around for something to throw at it, but when he turned again it was gone. He walked over to the balcony, but he could not see it anywhere.

The girl came back and sat down. He poured her out a glass of wine.

'Did you enjoy it?' he asked.

'Not much,' she said. 'I don't seem able to

195

enjoy anything these days.'

They were silent for a moment.

'Got drunk a couple of weeks ago,' he said suddenly in English, 'and tore a strip off one of the mess-waiters.'

'Why?' she asked.

'Oh, I don't know. I suppose it was the way he looked that irritated me. The crowd in the mess were up to their usual Saturday night fun and games – and he was looking daggers drawn.'

'Daggers drawn,' she repeated softly to herself, as if considering the phrase. 'What do you care?'

'I don't really. But I suddenly saw in him – a typical member of the working classes thinking what a lot of twerps we are. I suppose he's a communist or something.'

He took a drink of his wine.

'But what do they think they can do about it?'

'How do you mean?'

'Well, they think they can alter the world. And I suppose they can in a way. But they can't alter the important thing.'

'What's that?'

'Death! We're all going to kick the bucket one day. What the hell's the use of striving and reforming…' His voice trailed away.

After a while she said:

'Let's go for a drive – a fast drive!'

'O.K.,' he said, brightening suddenly.

They finished the wine and took another bottle with them down to the jeep. He took his trench-coat from the back and told her to put it on. 'Oh, yes,' he said, 'and I've got a badge for you. Stick it in the lapel,' he directed. 'If a M.P. patrol sees it they might think you're something to do with the army.'

They jolted and bumped their way slowly down the ruined, pot-holed roads out of town. Once he had to stop whilst a convoy of army lorries passed. Over to the left, on a ruined site, a group of ragged Germans stood round a wooden box upon which stood a British soldier. Behind him stood two or three people in Salvation Army uniform. The soldier was red-faced, fat, and wore pale horn-rimmed spectacles. He was haranguing his audience in English.

'...we get tired and blame others and get more tired. It was the same yesterday and it will be the same tomorrow. We're ashamed and we make it worse. Inspire in us healthy ones... Inspire in us suffering ones that we may be healed...'

'What next?' Green said aloud, and engaged his gear noisily.

They drove on. Once out in the country, Green put his foot down hard on the accelerator-pedal. The jeep jumped forward. Thirty – forty – fifty.

'Faster!' Gerda screamed above the roar of the wheels, exhilarated by the motion. The needle of the speedometer quivered up-wards. Sixty – seventy – eighty. Green had his foot down hard on the boards. The rubber of the wheels screeched and tore at the road. A fly hit the wind-screen like a bullet. Green opened his mouth slightly and felt the air flow in almost solidly. This was good, he told himself. If this could only go on for ever. The fir trees bordering the road flashed by – a patch of dark green. Up above the puffs of white clouds scudded by in the bright blue sky at a tremendous rate.

'Please God,' he prayed, 'let this go on for ever.'

They shuffled past in the dusk down the dusty, brick-littered street. Disembodied voices.

A harsh, coarse voice:

'Hold yer trap! What do I worry if the bulls are there!'

'But if they get me? I've got a wife and two kids. Please – you take them. I never wanted to start with the racket anyway.'

'Shut it! Rub yer fags in yer hair. Perhaps yer'll get curls if yer do. All I care about is the "moss", the "pinkie-pinke", the money – get it!'

'Ten cigarettes for the night, Tommie, Woodbines.'

An old woman's voice – persistent:

'And I tell yer that the lad doesn't get enough to eat. He won't live out the winter if he doesn't get something inside of him soon.'

'But what can I do, Mother? There's only bread and potatoes on the cards and...'

'Plenty of fat, that's what the lad needs. Give him a proper lining for the cold months.'

'But what can I do?'

'Well, there's plenty of Tommies about, aren't there? And yer don't still think that Erich's coming back, do you?'

'Ten cigarettes for the night, Tommie. Woodbines.'

Hopeful – a young woman's voice:

'I've saved ten pounds of apples and twenty cigarillos for him when he comes home. And the old 'un has let me have a jacket of his an' when he comes home I'll alter it...'

'But didn't you hear the one o'clock news?'

'No, what about it?'

'Well ... I don't like to be the one who has to tell you this ... but I suppose you'll have to know from someone. The Americans are sending all their prisoners over to the Russians to help with their reconstruction work...'

'Do you mean my Dieter?'

'Yes…'

'Ten cigarettes for the night, Tommie. Woodbines.'

'H'm, what is it? Gold?'

'Do you think I'd wear tin?'

'All right, but a bit old-fashioned. What do you want for it?'

'What do you think?'

'Well, you know how it is. Watches are hard to flog. Are you including the armband in the deal?'

'Yes.'

'What's this on the back – to Leutnant Georg Schneider on his eighteen birthday from Mutti. You officer?'

'How much'll you give me?'

'Five cigarettes for the night, Tommie.'

ILKA HARMANN

Ilka lay with her face on the table in the third-class waiting-room. She lay with her eyes closed, but she could not sleep although her body was exhausted. She had already spent four nights in the waiting-room, dodging outside every two hours when the police patrol came round looking at papers. And now, outside on the platform, she could hear the heavy tread of boots which heralded the approach of the patrol. But tonight she just could not force herself up and out of the other door. About her she could hear movement as the people who were living in the city without a pass, like herself, prepared to make their five minutes' walk around the platform until the patrol had gone. Then the police and their damned Alsatian were in the waiting-room. Somebody tapped on her shoulder, and she raised her head slowly – her eyes dazzled by the light of a torch thrust into her face.

'Papers – come on!' the policeman said, not even bothering to address her in the polite form. 'We've not got all night!'

She shook her head, a lock of hair falling in her face.

'Haven't got any,' she mumbled, all fight gone.

They took her away to the 'Revier' and released her next morning. The police sergeant at the desk was kindly, but firm.

'If you're brought in again, Fraulein,' he said. 'We'll have to send you back to Ivan. Got enough mouths to feed as it is.'

She hung her head, seeming not to hear his words. He looked at her severely for a moment, then fished in his brief-case which lay on the desk in front of him. He unfolded a grease-paper packet and handed her a small sandwich.

'Here you are,' he said. 'You're at liberty to go now.'

Without saying thank you, she shuffled outside into the grey morning. He looked after her for a moment, sadly, and then bent his head down to his reports again.

'Medical Report on Prisoner Ilka Harmann. Age 18. Domicile – unknown. Woman is pregnant and I suspect T.B. of both lungs.'

Outside in the gutter, Ilka took a bite at the sausage-sandwich the police sergeant had given her, but at the first bite she had to vomit in the gutter. Afterwards she leaned weakly against the wall of the 'Revier', but, although the occasional passer-by eyed her curiously, nobody stopped; they were hardened to sights such as these.

She dropped the liver-sausage sandwich in the dirt and staggered on. As she reached the corner, she remembered the sandwich and laboriously retraced her steps. Her pace quickened as she reached the spot where she had dropped it. For a moment, she thought, panic-stricken, that somebody had already found it, but it was only that the grey bread was hard to see against the dirt of the pavement. Carefully, she wiped the sandwich with the hem of her dress – as a mother might wipe the face of a baby – and ate it.

She staggered on, Ilka Harmann, daughter of Grossbauer Harmann; her hair hung lankily down her back, her face was puffy and wrinkled about the eyes from lack of sleep, and the sole of one of her shoes flapped up and down like a tongue every step she took.

Painfully, she made her way to the bar where she had been employed. It was early, and the chairs were still stacked upon the little tables. The cleaner was washing the floor, but Ilka had not the strength to go round the freshly-washed part. The cleaner was about to say something to her sharply, but when she saw the look in Ilka's face she desisted. Ilka went on without even seeing her.

The manager looked fatter and greasier than ever. She told him she would like her job back. He pressed the bare leg of the young boy in short leather trousers who sat upon the arm of his chair and said:

'My God! No, you certainly can't come back. I lost a very dear young friend to that damned farmer through you. And, besides, look at yourself!' He pointed to the mirror, but she did not look. As she went out, the manager pressed the young boy's knee lovingly, and they laughed.

She wandered around the rest of that day in a daze. Once or twice she was tempted to ask somebody for food, but after a time her hunger seemed to disappear. Towards evening, she was threading her way unsteadily through dim-lit ruined streets behind the station looking for somewhere to sleep in the rubble, when she heard a drunken voice behind her.

'Hey, Fraulein, wait for me!'

She stopped and supported herself against a twisted gas lamp. A tall soldier with three stripes on his arm staggered up to her. When he spoke, he breathed beer all over her. He said something which she did not understand.

'Well,' he said. 'Yes or no?'

She shook her head in a weary gesture, which he took for assent. Seizing her arm in his, he staggered off down the middle of the ruined street.

He took her to his room, but did not turn on the light until he had drawn the blackout curtains. He kept putting his finger to his lips to indicate that she should be quiet, although he blundered around himself making a great deal of noise. In one corner of the room she saw an army cot, and she went over to it and collapsed on it. He took a deep swig from the open bottle on the table, and began to get undressed. Far in the distance, as if in another world, she could hear him grunt as he bent down to take off his boots. Then he turned and threaded his way in the dark to the bed and got in beside her. Clumsily he fumbled with her clothes and began to undress her. He could not undo the catch of her dress, and, suddenly losing patience, he tore it off her – and she let it happen.

CLAUSEN

The thought of what he would do to the judge who had sentenced him to death that day in April had always been one of Clausen's pleasantest thoughts during the last few months. And now he had the man in front of him, and he did not do a thing. In fact, he was scared. He was hungry, and he needed a job badly – especially a job in a British camp where he might get scraps from the kitchen. A comrade he had asked at the petrol pump had told him they needed drivers in the motor pool, and he had gone to the British labour office, and now he was faced with the judge – or the interpreter, as he was now.

The interpreter clamped his pince-nez more firmly on his nose, and looked down at the papers. Oh, please God, let him give me the job – and don't let him ask for my permit. Oh, please God… Clausen prayed fervently.

'So you would like a job with the British Occupation Power, would you?' he said, as if he personally were the 'British Occupation Power'.

'Yes … sir.'

The interpreter smiled softly.

'You don't need to call me sir,' he said. 'Those days are – thank God – gone for ever. You – we – must realize that in a democracy things are different.'

He looked at Clausen.

'I seem to know your face,' he said. 'Were you in the army? Officer?'

Clausen was about to say 'leutnant', but decided 'private' was safer.

'Just an ordinary soldier, sir,' he said, keeping his eyes lowered.

The interpreter did not object to the 'sir' this time.

'Hm,' he said, and tapped his middle finger against his lip. 'All right,' he said. 'You can start tomorrow in the motor pool. You get two hundred a month and one free meal. Is that all right with you?'

'Yes, sir. But couldn't I possibly start today, sir? I haven't had anything to eat … and I thought–'

The interpreter interrupted him.

'Look here. We must start on a proper understanding. We Germans must show the British that we can do as we are told. We say we start on Tuesday, and we start on Tuesday, and not Wednesday or Thursday. Order – that's what we must have. Got it?… You're a soldier. You must have learnt how to curb your hunger. I remember when I still wore the uniform of the… But no matter. Start tomorrow.'

He waved a hand. Clausen was dismissed. Thank God, he whispered as he went through the door. He didn't recognize me. He didn't ask for my permit. Thank God.

He was given a job driving a jeep in the motor pool. He had to drive visiting officers and personnel of officer rank who had permission to use military transport. He drove all types of officers in the next few days, and liked it, though the conversation with most of them did not go past the stage of:

'In the German army? What did you think of the Russians? Were you a Nazi? Used to think they had some good ideas myself before the war. Do you think you could get me a Leica?'

That was until he got the job of driving Mrs Smythe around. She was a Red Cross worker, who had just come out to the 'Zone', as they called it among themselves, as if it were a part of India. Mrs Smythe was in her late thirties and her hair was already going grey, though she tinted it every night with cold tea because she could not get any hair dye in the 'Zone' and she did not feel like having it sent through the censor.

Her husband was a regular officer somewhere out East, whom she had not seen for four years. During the war, she had assisted in canteens and other welfare establishments in the London area. For a time she had run a small canteen at a large station, handing out tea and jam-jars – because 'you men always break the cups' – to British soldiers passing through. But as soon as it was decently possible she had herself transferred to a canteen serving foreign troops. The British soldier, with his scruffy, untidy appearance and the inevitable cigarette end stuck behind his ear, she found vulgar and ungrateful. The foreign troops were different, especially the Americans. In the winter of 1942, she was sleeping with an American top-sergeant – at that time her husband was ploughing his way back through the Burmese jungle to India.

By the end of 1944 she had worked her way up to a general in the Eighth Air Force, who was not virile, but was nice to have around, in spite of his habit of sitting around in his underwear and boots, smoking a cigar. But the war came to an end, and she decided she had to make a break, so she came out to the 'Zone'. She accepted an occasional gin in the mess, but she retired early and did not attend the 'Open Night'. They referred to her as 'that rather nice Mrs Smythe' in the mess, and the colonel, who had put his hand on her knee one night in the mess when he was drunk, could not meet her eye the next morning.

But the itch was still there. And, as she went about her business that August, she gradually became aware of the broad back of her driver, Clausen. She took to sitting in the front with him and leaving a packet of cigarettes or a bar of chocolate in the cubbyhole in the dash-board. It would be quite some fun, she decided one day. Forbidden fruits always taste the sweetest. She was amused and thrilled at the idea. Wonder if I should hold a record for being the first Englishwoman since the war to let a German... She stopped, because she never used the vulgar words even to herself.

She planned her campaign of seduction; it was not for nothing that she was a regular officer's wife. She had the cook make her up a huge parcel of sandwiches and bought two bottles of wine at the mess. Then she got Clausen to drive her down the estuary one fine morning. She had already conceived the situation. She would find one of those fine, sandy dunes well away from the main road, and get him to stop. She would say she wanted to stretch her legs, and get out of the car. Then, as if she had suddenly come to a decision, she would tell him to bring the sandwiches and wine across and invite him to drink with her. He would be humble and very grateful. Later, she would stretch out in the hot sun and let the sun beat down on her face for a time. And he would take off his shirt – she remembered the muscular bodies of the Germans sunbathing at the pools before the war. Suddenly, she would run her fingers through his hair, as if she could not help herself. And then he would… She imagined a young man's heavy muscular body. It gave her a delightful thrill. I hope he's brown all over, she prayed to herself. Afterwards, he would be terribly grateful and perhaps they could do something about sleeping together – her room was on the ground floor overlooking the cobbled courtyard. She imagined what it would be like in the great double bed she had in her room. It didn't creak – she'd tested it. Her legs seemed to turn to water as she thought about it. But it did not turn out that way. For one thing it rained, and for another the driver knew more than she suspected. There was a certain cynical bitterness about him which destroyed her mood, which demanded youthful innocence on the part of the partner.

They were in a typical half-timbered German barn, sheltering from the rain, which was coming down in torrents. She was annoyed by the rain, but still, there were possibilities in the barn, she thought, and her eye swept round its interior quickly, noting the pile of hay in the corner. They stood in the doorway watching the rain, and she shivered, as if she were cold. He did not seem to notice, but stared on into the rain, which sweep down the front of the barn in sheets.

'It's very lonely here,' she said, invitation

in her voice.

'There are some houses down the way, Mrs Smythe,' he said, slurring the 'th' in her name ever so slightly.

They were silent.

'You were in Russia?' she said, breaking the silence.

He nodded his head.

'What are the Russian women like?'

'I did not see many at the front,' he said. 'There were no women in the Kampf-gebieten...' He shrugged his shoulders. 'I do not know the word in English. Away from the front I saw some. Big girls – very clean – the peasants, at least. Didn't like the Germans much – after the first months.'

She had hoped to get him talking about women, which was always a good start, but he dried up.

As a last hope she went and lay down in the hay, stretching her arms back over her head so that her breasts would press forward through the thin material of her khaki shirt. She had heard that the Germans liked to get hold of a handful in their women.

'Why don't you come and sit down here?' she said, with false gaiety. 'It's nice and warm in the hay.'

He half-turned, and shook his head.

'No, thank you, Mrs Smythe,' he said. 'A thousand calories a day does not permit it.'

He remained standing at the door, staring

into the rain.

She gave up and relaxed her body, feeling her breasts sink flaccid and soft. Wonder what he meant about a 'thousand calories a day', she asked herself.

The British provided their civilian employees with a mid-day meal – usually pea soup and a slice of stale bread left over from the other ranks' cookhouse, or 'Soya Link' sausages which the men would not eat. The German civilian employees saw that in the English cookhouse there was a certain fixed scale of privileges, whereby the sergeant-cook was allowed to sell the rations on a large scale to the officers and his fellow N.C.O.s, the corporal-cook the occasional joint of meat or pound of sugar, and the orderlies, what was left over at the end of the day from the men's food. This system they compared with that of their own cookhouse, where the interpreter, who was in charge – a certain Schmidt, former major in the German army – claimed the sole right to any surplus food. ·

As the summer wore on and food became progressively scarcer, the German employees felt that they, too, ought to have a share in the surplus food from their mess. Clausen, who had been transferred to the mess as an orderly, was elected as the staff's representative to see the interpreter.

'You're an educated man,' they said. 'You know how to tackle his type better than we can. Why should that beer-belly (meaning Schmidt) have all the leavings? He sits there on his fat bottom in the office, and we do all the graft. He doesn't work in the cook-house!'

'But you've more right to go than me,' Clausen protested. 'I'm only an orderly.'

'Don't be silly, man,' they laughed, and slapped him on the back. 'You're one of us, man. Don't worry – we're backing you up. You're our representative.'

So Clausen went. Schmidt sat behind his desk outside the adjutant's office, reading his papers. He did not look up when Clausen came in, but remained bent over his papers. After what seemed ages to Clausen, he grunted, without looking up.

'Well?'

It was disconcerting, but Clausen did faithfully what he had to do.

'Herr Schmidt... I've been sent by the rest of the kitchen personnel.' He paused.

'Hurry up, man,' Schmidt grunted. 'I've no time to waste.'

'Well, sir,' Clausen went on hurriedly. 'We think that all the leavings and extras in the kitchen should be shared equally among the lot of us and not ... well ... you should not have it all for yourself.'

Schmidt looked up with an interested

213

smile on his face. Though inside he was scared. Hope to Christ that the adjutant doesn't come out now, he told himself.

'Hm,' he said. 'So that's what they say, is it?' He looked at Clausen in his ragged, greasy Denim fatigues, that had been given to him by one of the cooks. 'And you're their representative, are you?' He pronounced the word 'representative' with a certain amount of scorn. 'Representative, eh?' He toyed with the word. 'I'm glad to see you adopted such a democratic procedure so quickly.' He yawned. 'Go back and tell them that there's nothing doing.'

Clausen began to protest.

'But, sir, surely you can't use all the scraps for yourself? Some of the people in the kitchen have children...'

The interpreter held up his hand for silence.

'Close the door after you when you go out,' he said shortly.

Clausen let his shoulders droop. He knew it was no use. Let somebody else have a go, he told himself. He was no good in slanging matches with officials. Never had been. He moved to the door and was about to go out when Schmidt spoke.

'Oh, by the way, what is your name, please?'

'Clausen,' he said briefly.

'Thank you.'

214

As he closed the door, he had the impression that Schmidt was writing something.

A moment after Clausen left, the interpreter went in to the adjutant with papers for signing in his hand. Dutifully the adjutant signed them without bothering to read those that were in German.

'Don't know how you get your tongue round it,' he had once admitted to the interpreter. 'I wouldn't be able to learn it, if you gave me a hundred pounds.'

One of the papers was a notice of dismissal for one, Friedrich Clausen. Reason for dismissal: absence of residence permit.

When Clausen told them that he had been sacked, they gathered round him with serious faces. He took off his fatigues and began to roll them, but they held his hand and stopped him.

'Don't do that, man,' they said. 'You'll be needing them again today.'

'Yes,' somebody else said. 'Now you're going to see an example of working-class solidarity in action.'

'That's right,' one of the maids said. 'We'll see you get your job back, Mr Clausen, or they'll have to sack the lot of us.'

'Ay,' they echoed, 'or they'll have to sack the lot of us.'

That afternoon, after three o'clock tea had been served in the mess, they went in a bunch to the interpreter's office. He was startled when he saw them come in. Thank God the adjutant's not in this afternoon, he told himself. But his fear did not show on his face. He smiled and got to his feet.

'Good afternoon,' he said. 'Glad to see you all.'

They had expected him to ask then why they had come, but he did not, and they were put off balance. He began to arrange chairs in a half-circle round his desk. He waved his hand at them.

'Please sit down,' he said. 'I expect you've been on your feet enough today already.'

They hesitated for a moment.

'What we've come to say to you...' somebody began. Then, Waldtraut, whose feet hurt like hell, sat down heavily. The others followed suit.

The interpreter opened the drawer of his desk and took out a packet of twenty Players.

'Let's have a Tommi for a change,' he said, and handed the packet to Emil. He hesitated, but he had not had a smoke for eight hours, and after a moment he took one. The cigarettes went the rounds.

There was a moment's silence.

'We've come to see you about Clausen—' somebody began, but Schmidt interrupted.

'My goodness,' he said heartily. 'Do make yourself comfortable. Sit back in your chairs. You are sitting there so stiffly.' He smiled. 'In

216

this day and age I hope we have forgotten the old boss and employee relationship. I only regret that I haven't as much time as I would wish to make myself acquainted with your work. But I tell you, I will certainly make the time in future.

'Now, what can I do for you, ladies and gentlemen?'

'Well, it's like this–' somebody began, but again Schmidt interrupted. His eyes twinkled.

'I think,' he said, drawing the words out, 'I've got something for the ladies, too, although I can see that you're smoking. Well,' he shrugged his shoulders, 'those days are past when it was considered immoral for a woman to smoke, aren't they?'

He opened his drawer again and took out a box of chocolates. 'Sweets for the sweet,' he said. 'An officer gave it to me yesterday … and what could I do with chocolates?' He laughed.

He opened the box and held it out invitingly at the maids. They looked at each other, and then Waldtraut dipped her hand in and took out a chocolate. The other one followed suit. 'Well, just one,' she said.

'And now, gentlemen,' Schmidt said, and smiled. 'Now something for more masculine tastes.' He began to rummage in his desk.

Two hours later, he had them eating out of his hand. Emil had already been sick from eating chocolate and drinking cognac on an empty stomach, and one of the maids was sitting on the cook's knee.

'Clausen,' the interpreter was saying, 'came to me, but he didn't say anything about being your representative. He suggested – one might almost say threatened – that he wanted half the food that comes from the cookhouse, or else! I explained the situation to him – and that from next week onwards the food is going to be divided equally between all the kitchen personnel. But he wouldn't listen. I sacked him on the spot–'

'The dirty rat!' Emil interrupted. 'He didn't tell us that.'

'Yes,' the others agreed. 'What a dirty rat!'

'Come on, gentlemen,' the interpreter said. 'A man can't stand on one leg alone. What about another drink?'

Clausen waited for them for hours in the kitchen. He looked at the wall-clock. They ought to be starting dinner now, he told himself, and then they came in. As they saw him, they lowered their eyes, but their flushed faces told him all he wanted to know. Quietly, he began to roll up his overalls.

JIMMIE

Jimmie had the kitchen to himself. He was on late turn. In half an hour's time he would have to take the big brown pots of tea and

218

the plates of fish sandwiches – to give the officers a thirst – into the mess for the buffet supper. But at the moment he had nothing to do. He had washed, shaved and fried himself an egg, and now he was trying to get down to some writing. In front of him he had an old Tauchnitz dictionary, which he had bought recently for a few cigarettes, and a German newspaper. He was trying to decipher an article about a new type of skin disease that was affecting a great number of people. It was a large sore which appeared on the arms, legs and head, and which after treatment seemed to heal, yet broke out again on another part of the body a few days later; it was thought to be due to mal-nutrition. 'Keineswegs ansteckend', he read. He did not know what the words meant, and he started to thumb his way through the dog-eared dictionary. It stuck him that if he could somehow dramatize the article – perhaps a word-picture of a kid with these 'places' as the Jerries called them – it would make a good contrast to the scene where Greenaway, the main character, is mugging himself in the mess. He found out what 'ansteckend' meant, and was about to carry on when the door from the mess opened and Green came in. Jimmie jumped up and stood to attention. He could tell from Green's manner that he was drunk. Stewed as a newt, he told himself.

Green did not say anything for a minute – just stood looking at him.

'Get me a cup of coffee – black!' he said thickly.

Jimmie felt angry. What the hell does he think I am? he thought. A bloody wet-nurse!

'I'll be serving sandwiches and tea in the mess in half an hour's time, sir,' he said.

Green looked at him fixedly for a second.

'Firstly,' he said, 'I don't want tea, but coffee. And secondly, I want it now.'

'The Mess President said–' Jimmie began, but Green interrupted him.

'I know what the Mess President said. Let him be my worry. You just go and do that nice, simple job.' He spoke as if to a child. 'Do as you're told.'

Jimmie shrugged his shoulders angrily and went over to the stove. Green slumped down heavily into the kitchen chair. It was forbidden for officers to come into the kitchen, Jimmie knew, but it was no use telling Green that in his present condition.

Whilst Jimmie busied himself at the stove, Green toyed idly with the paper on the table.

'Do you flog much stuff here?' he asked disinterestedly.

'Not much,' Jimmie answered as cheekily as he dared.

The officer did not seem to hear. He was staring down at the paper in front of him.

Slowly he began to read from it:

'Lieutenant Greenaway licked the butter from his fingers carefully so that no one in the mess saw him, and looked out of the window at the shabby crowd of Germans that thronged the streets outside. The crowd irritated him somehow or other, and he clicked his fingers in my direction.

'"Draw the curtains," he said. "The sight of them destroys one's appetite."

'I did as I was told and went back to my place near the wall. I watched him as he ate. The first thing that struck one about his face was its curious blank look, his eyes especially, which were dulled over like a bright pan in a jet of steam. The first time I had seen him he had looked like that. It was just before the fighting in the Falaise Gap. He was walking down the road with a Luger in his hand, and a few yards behind him came his batman telling everyone that he, Greenaway, had just shot a Pole who had wanted to surrender. He had done it – for the kick he got out of it. For the kick he got out of it – those were the batman's words...'

The officer stopped reading and looked at Jimmie, who had turned round at the stove.

'Green – Greenaway – Green,' the officer muttered. 'Who wrote that?'

'Me,' Jimmie said after a moment's hesitation, omitting the 'sir'.

The officer tugged the end of his nose.

221

'So that's how you see me,' he said slowly. 'What was it you said?... "To see if he could get a kick out of it".'

'It's not exactly you,' Jimmie said.

'But that with the Pole...'

'Yes, sir,' Jimmie said hesitantly. 'That's you, but the character is more a composite creation of my experience and—'

'Those are very big words you're using,' Green interrupted, somewhat amused. 'What was it we used to say as kids? – have you swallowed a dictionary?'

Jimmie flushed.

'It doesn't mean because a bloke left school at fourteen he has to stick to words of one syllable!' he blurted out.

The officer held up his hands in mock alarm.

'Oh, my dear man. Please don't get excited. I don't want to cast any doubts on your intellectual ability. But after six years in the army and all that...' He left the sentence unfinished. He did not speak again until Jimmie set the coffee down in front of him on the table. 'So you're going to be a writer,' he said.

'Yes,' Jimmie said, and bent down to remove the papers from in front of the officer, but he shook his head and Jimmie desisted.

'Why?'

'Because ... I want to.'

'Hm, and what are you going to write

about? Do you think the reading public – as I believe they are called – will find me interesting?'

'I don't know, sir. I hope so.'

The officer looked down at the papers and sipped the hot black coffee.

'Go and get me a measure of brandy from the bar,' he said, without looking up. 'I'll sign the chitty.'

Jimmie threw a hopeless glance at the papers and went out. When he came back, Green took the glass of brandy from him and poured its contents into his coffee.

'When you make your pile,' he said, 'you'll be able to do that too.'

Jimmie went red.

Green looked up and tapped the papers with one finger slowly.

'Listen to this,' he said. '"Joe spoke: 'It's about time that shower back home got their skates out. If they'd have been faced with this sort of lark,' and he swept his arm round in a circle to embrace the ruined centre of the city, 'they'd have turned up their toes and given the daisies a treat. I remember once when I was in the grubber before this last do...'"'

Green stopped reading. 'What do you call that?'

'What do you mean, sir?'

'Well, the style first ... and then words like "grubber" and "do" and down here' – he

223

pointed at the page with his forefinger – '"slaver". You surely can't hope to get that sort of stuff published! And besides, who's going to be interested in that sort of person? Who'd give a damn about what happened to Mike, or Joe, or whatever the devil you call the feller. I think I can say I'm pretty well read in Modern English Literature, but I can't say I've ever come across this sort of thing very often.'

'Don't you think it's about time, then, that someone did start writing about people like Joe? Perhaps we–'

Green cut him short impatiently. 'But haven't you realized yet,' he said, 'that ordinary people are boring – that is, working-class people? You might feel it's terribly important. A message, and all that sort of bilge. But is it really? You can write until you're blue in the face, but you can't alter the only important thing – that we're all going to be dead in fifty or sixty years' time. You're always faced with that, and you can't do a sausage about it. Give the people something to take their minds off that and you're made.'

'I don't give a damn what people want...' Jimmie blurted out, and then stopped suddenly as he saw the slow smile spread across Green's face. He knew what Green was thinking, and it hurt.

There was silence. Green finished his

coffee and got up slowly.

'Bring me the chitty pad,' he said, and, as an afterthought – 'Please.'

Jimmie went into the mess again and brought the pad. Green signed for a cognac and, with the pencil poised in his hand, he said:

'Have a beer on me?'

The request was more than just a question of having or not having a glass of beer, Jimmie realized that, but he shook his head.

'No thank you, sir,' he said. 'I'm not keen on beer.'

Green shrugged his shoulders. 'All right,' he said slowly. 'All right.'

Go and jump off a cliff, Jimmie thought. I can always go in the cellar and whip a bottle if I want. You can't buy me with your damn beer.

Green looked at him for a minute, and then walked to the door. He turned.

'Well,' he said, 'if you ever do get it published, you'd better watch out. I might sue you for the character of Greenaway.' He laughed, and the door swung to behind him. Jimmie sat down at his papers. The top page had a circle of coffee where Green had rested his cup upon it. Jimmie picked up the page as carefully as he could, but the coffee began to run down. He stood up and walked over to the window where the slops pail was kept, and threw it in. As he did so, he noticed a black mangy dog that was sitting outside in the rain, looking at the house mournfully.

'That stumer Green,' he said half-aloud, and went back to his seat again.

GREEN

It was the afternoon of the next day that the colonel informed them that the Regiment would be going to the Far East in the very near future as soon as transportation for the Division's vehicles could be secured. Green went out promptly and got drunk in the mess.

He climbed unsteadily into the jeep and engaged the gear noisily. Somebody had turned the gramophone on and was playing the damned 'Bella, Bella Maria' record again, he thought.

He started the jeep with a jerk and lurched forward. He stalled the motor and had to start it again. With the stupid thoroughness of the very drunk he lifted his foot very, very slowly off the pedal.

So this is it, he thought, as he drove very slowly through the deserted streets of the ruined city. Somehow he could not see himself out East. He wondered what Gerda would say. Carefully, he parked the jeep behind the heap of rubble near Gerda's place, chained it securely to an iron railing and removed the rotor arm. If they pinch the wheels, he told himself, it's just too bad.

He began to climb the stairs slowly. It was somewhat of a feat to climb the stairs in the pitch darkness – even for a sober man. The stairs and the inner wall were the only remaining parts left standing of the two lower floors of the bombed house in which Gerda lived all by herself. The house was like a stripped cabbage leaf after the caterpillars have finished with it. Gerda's room – if one could call it a room – was just a large tarpaulin draped between the two inner walls and hanging down on one side, where a pile of loose bricks provided a kind of a wind-break. Every time one walked across the floor – avoiding the large hole in the middle of it – the bricks rattled and threatened to fall. Of course, it was unsafe, but so were many of the places in which people lived that summer. At all events, it was better than living in the bunker, she had often told him.

Green knocked on the rickety door and went in. Gerda was sitting on the bed, reading by the light of a candle. She looked up, surprised to see him.

'Hello,' she said. 'I didn't know you were coming tonight. I thought you had a mess dinner.'

Green nodded his head in affirmation.

'We had, but I dodged out.' He did not say anything more, but unwrapped the package he had under his arm. 'Couldn't get much,' he said. 'Just a couple of tins of corned beef and a white loaf, and there are some sandwiches left over from last night. 'Fraid they're stale.'

She got off the bed and began eating the sandwiches.

'Had nothing to eat, today,' she said by way of explanation.

'But what about that extra ration card I got you?' he said.

'They haven't honoured the ration cards this week yet,' she said shortly.

He pulled a bottle out of each pocket. Her face lit up.

'My spirit ration,' he said.

'I thought you'd had it for this month,' she said, surprised.

'Yes, I have. But this is next month's.'

'How come?'

'Well, we're … leaving next month and I thought that…'

'You're going?' She did not turn round, but stopped eating her sandwich with it poised half-eaten close to her open mouth.

'Yes,' he said. 'Out East.'

Mechanically, she began to eat the stale sandwich again.

'Out East,' she repeated dully.

They had finished the bottle of whisky and were starting on the gin, drinking it neat because he had forgotten to bring a bottle of cordial. She filled her glass and drank it down with a shudder.

He laughed. 'I'm well away,' he said.

'Ex!' she said, and finished the rest of her glass without waiting to see if he had lifted his glass.

'So this is about it,' she said in English.

'Yes,' he repeated. 'This is about it. It will be on Regimental Orders tomorrow, and after that we can move at any time.'

'Do you want to go?'

He wondered if she wanted him to say 'no' because of her.

'No,' he said. 'Not particularly. About all I want to do now is to get drunk and stay drunk as long as is humanly possible.'

He filled the glasses again and raised his. 'So saying,' he said, 'he took an overdose of extract of barley and knew no pain for three days.'

She did not laugh, because she did not understand him.

'You like to get drunk,' she said.

'So do you.'

'Yes, but in a different way from you. If I get drunk it usually makes me happy and I forget. With you it's different. You remain pretty much the same.'

'Perhaps you're right,' he said, after a moment's silence. 'It seems to me that I've spent a great deal of my life being and getting drunk.'

'If you could,' she asked, trying another tack. 'Would you like to have your life over again?'

'I don't know. Looking back, I don't think I've ever been different from what I am now. If you take a long-term view of life. Compare the length of your life with the life of the Universe as a whole... Aw come on. Let's have another drink!'

'Ex.'

'Ex.'

They drank some more, and after a while he left the rickety chair upon which he was sitting and moved over to the bed beside her. He kissed her, and suddenly she pressed his head hard against her breasts. He had known other women do this, but never Gerda. There was an aggressiveness about her love-making that night that was usually lacking. He could not account for it.

Afterwards, she lay awake and looked at the night sky where the tarpaulin had slipped, with her hands folded underneath her head on the pillow. Ever since he had told her that he was going, the idea had been forming in her head, and now she was decided. She wondered if he would do it with her. There was not much for it but that, she told herself. When he went, it would be pretty much the end. She turned and kissed him gently on the forehead. She could not remember a time for years that she had been so tranquil and content as tonight. She wakened him.

He blinked his eyes rapidly several times and rubbed the back of his hand against his scummed lips.

'Give me a drink,' he mumbled. In silence she poured him out a drink. After a while, she suggested that they should go for a drive. He looked at his watch, and seem about to refuse.

'Oh, all right,' he said. 'It's nearly one. The M.P. patrols will be off the roads now.'

She felt quite sober and enjoyed the cool air outside as she helped him out into the street. He was about to climb behind the wheel, but she steered him round to the other seat.

'I'll drive,' she said.

'I didn't know you could,' he muttered, and slumped in the other seat.

It was fresh, and she pulled the collar of her thin, white summer coat tight against her neck as they cruised slowly through the deserted night streets. Funny, she thought, as they passed the ruins. I grew up here and can't even recognize the place. Everything's just another ruin.

Green's brain raced wildly, yet his thoughts had a clarity and sharpness of perception that sometimes accompanies drunkenness. He slumped back in the iron bucket seat and watched the black ruins silhouetted against the night sky. So this is it, he thought. This is the end of it all – a heap of rubble and twisted girders in a foreign city.

Once clear of the ruined suburbs of the city, she pressed the accelerator down hard against the floorboards and they sped along the smooth tarmac of the road. Green was fascinated by the nervous quickening of the luminous needle of the speedometer as it moved up along its arc – 30 – 40 – 50. It was as if it were the last thing alive on the earth apart from himself.

The sound of the wheels burning up the road seemed to take possession of her ears and gave her a mighty feeling of power. It was then that she spotted the corner. At the speed she was travelling, she never had a chance to consider whether she would or would not. She gave the wheel a quick jerk to the right and they went crashing through the wooden fence. For a moment she had a sensation of sailing powerfully through air, and then they began to fall.

CHAPTER VI

SEPTEMBER

...We shall march on
When everything lies in ruins!
For today Germany is ours,
And tomorrow the whole world!

Horst Wessel Song.

It grew cold and started to rain. And they began to worry about the coming winter. In one street they organized themselves into working parties and began to dig in the ruins in search of buried coal. They began to offer fabulous prices for an army blanket, which they made into a kind of greatcoat everyone would seem to be wearing that winter. Whenever they could, they bought and hoarded a tin of margarine or corned-beef.

At night they went into the woods and chopped down the trees secretly for fuel for the winter. They even stole the trees from the big boulevards in the Town Centre. It was the time for turnips, and the women spent whole days boiling huge pans full of turnips in order to make a kind of black syrup which would store for the winter.

The summer was departing, and the urgency of winter was making itself felt. Everywhere in the streets one saw the bowed figures of old women in black, pulling heavy loads of twigs and branches in their trek-carts behind them.

The truck stood in the centre of the narrow road with the engine ticking over. The driver honked his horn violently.

'Get that bloody cart off the road, can't yer?' he shouted at the old woman.

She looked up at him, with tears in her eyes.

'Ich kann nicht,' she said. 'Das Rad ist kaput. The wheel is kaput.'

'Too bad,' the driver snapped, and put the truck noisily into gear. With a splintering crash, he hit the little cart and sent the twigs and branches flying into the ditch.

JIMMIE

They were the B.L.A. – British Liberation Army – but they joked among themselves about the initials meaning 'Burma Looms Ahead'. Most of them were scared of going out to the East to fight the Japs – they had seen too many films about them. When the Mountain Artillery Battery had left the Division for India in March, they had talked about it in hushed tones usually reserved for major catastrophes. And now it was happening to them. Charlie and Jimmie packed up in the cookhouse there and then. The corporal-cook protested, but they told him what to do with his mess. Anyway, the officers were doing exactly what they intended to do – getting drunk.

Like most of the men in the Regiment, they headed for the 'out of bounds' cafés where there were women and drink. The place they went into was full of men from the Regiment and other regiments of the Division – and girls. They sat down and ordered a bottle of Schnapps. It cost them 300 marks. They gave the waiter seventy-five cigarettes. A couple of girls floated in their direction, but Charlie waved them away.

'Let's concentrate on some serious boozing,' he said. 'I want to be real stewed before I start thinking about bits of frat.'

Jimmie nodded, and poured out a couple of drinks.

'Here's mud in yer eye,' he said, and raised his glass.

'Up your gonga,' Charlie said, and raised his. 'What's it these Jerries say – gleic – gleic.'

'Gleichfalls,' Jimmie finished it for him.

'Yes, that's it,' Charlie said. 'I was just getting hold of the lingo.'

They drank, and the raw spirit made even Charlie cough.

'Christ!' he said. 'What do they put in this stuff – paraffin!' He shrugged his shoulders. 'Don't care if I do go blind.'

'Did you know,' Jimmie asked conversationally, 'that the Brylcreem boys drink petrol and grapefruit juice?'

'Nope.'

In the rest of the city, incidents between civilians and the members of the outgoing Division were mounting. Already there were some thirty soldiers being held in the Town Guard-Room for rape and armed assault. The Divisional Provost Marshal was worried – it reminded him of the time back in '42 when the Australians got out of hand and burned down the brothels. Reports were coming in from all sides of soldiers beating up the unarmed German police, stripping the frocks from girls in the streets, holding up cafés for spirits. There had already been two cases of soldiers striking N.C.O.s. He decided to ask for police reinforcements from Corps.

They raked together the remainder of their cigarettes and ordered another bottle. They had been joined by some soldiers from their former troop – the Anti-Tank – and the first two bottles had gone pretty quickly.

'Charlie,' Jimmie said above the din about them. 'I'm going to go over the hill.'

'What!' Charlie said, surprised. 'On the

236

trot! What for?'

Jimmie thought for a moment. 'I'm sick of the army,' he said. 'And, besides, I want to stay here.'

'But listen here,' Charlie protested. 'You know what happens if you desert on active service. Remember Smithie who took a powder in Holland. He got three years in the Nick for it.'

'Yes, I know,' Jimmie said. 'But I'm blowing all the same. I'm sick of the whole bloody show. I might go over to the Russkies like Big Ram Jones in B Company.'

Charlie replenished the glasses. 'Come on. Drink up,' he said. 'You've got the hump like a lot of us, but you'll forget it. Wait till we're kipping up with them Geisha girls.'

Jimmie laughed.

'Yer and my Aunt Fanny's me Uncle Joe,' he answered.

Charlie waved over some of the girls, and they shuffled back in their chairs to make room for them. Charlie gave them all a drink and a cigarette. Jimmie just sat there drinking and listening idly to their chatter. He thought of his wife and kid. What would happen to them if he deserted? he wondered. They would lose their allowance, he supposed. Oh, what did he care, he thought savagely. If you wanted to achieve anything in this world, you had to be hard and ride roughshod over other people. What did he owe them, or anybody else for that matter? Nobody had ever done anything for him. The only thing he wanted to do was to write. He didn't give a damn for the rest of the world.

He realized that he was sweating, and took a deep drink of his Schnapps. At the bar they started to sing:

Drunk last night. Drunk the night before.

Shock the world, he muttered fiercely under his breath, and the thought hammered its way home in his brain.

Gonna get drunk tonight like we've never been drunk before.

Shock the world! Shock the world! Shock the world!

Glory be to God. There isn't any more of us,
Because one of us could drink the bloody lot.

They tried to get the owner to keep the place open, but it was long after curfew and he had run out of drink, so he would not. They threw a few empty bottles about and smashed the large mirror behind the bar, and then they left.

Outside, it was dark and cold and the girls shivered. They stood there – about twenty men and girls – when a Dingo followed by an armoured car came slowly round the corner. A searchlight was switched on and swept the road from left to right. At the same time, a voice kept repeating mechanically through a loudspeaker: 'It is now twenty-three, thirty hours. All British other ranks will now leave the streets. It is now twenty-three, thirty hours...'

Somebody sneered. The searchlight swept over them, and then came back, like a living thing coming back to have another look.

'Are those German civilians?' the disembodied voice asked.

'Lose yourself,' Charlie shouted into the light which blinded them. The girls were frightened.

'I repeat,' the voice said, 'Are those German civilians?'

'Yer,' somebody shouted, 'an' what yer gonna do about it?'

The searchlight swung away and the two vehicles turned slowly and crossed the road. A British officer and sergeant came across to them, and five or six M.P.s jumped out noisily on to the road and stood there waiting.

'Are you German?' the officer asked the nearest girl in broken German.

She nodded her head.

'All right, Sergeant,' he said. 'Curfew breakers. Take them in.'

The sergeant waved to the waiting M.P.s and then started leading the girl who had spoken over to the armoured car. The men murmured among themselves, and one soldier took hold of the sergeant's arm.

'Hey,' he said. 'You can't do that. That's my bint.'

'Can't I?' the sergeant said, and gave him a punch with his free hand in the stomach which doubled him up.

The officer, who had been about to return to the Dingo, turned round and let his hand slide down significantly to the holster of his thirty-eight. 'That's enough of that...'

'But he's taken my bint,' the man who had been hit in the stomach persisted.

'I said that's enough of that.' He tapped the holster. 'There's been just enough trouble with you men in this town tonight. Save it for the Japs.'

He clicked his fingers, and the searchlight was brought to bear upon them again. They blinked and lowered their eyes.

'Right,' he said, 'I can see you quite clearly now. If you've got anything to say – say it. Otherwise, be off back to your billets.'

In the light of the searchlight, they could see that the Besa, mounted on the Dingo, was pointed in their direction. Slowly they moved away, the searchlight followed them the whole time like an accusing finger. As they got round the corner out of reach of the searchlight, they stopped, undecided what to do. In the distance, they could hear someone crying. One or two of them muttered to themselves, but Charlie stopped them.

'All right,' he snapped. 'Put a sock in it. You know what we're gonna do? We're gonna get them Frauleins back.'

'How yer gonna do that, Charlie?' somebody asked. 'Them M.P.s are in a bad mood.'

'Aw, if yer windy, yer better take a powder now,' Charlie said, disgusted.

'You can go and...' the man who had spoken began.

'Blow it out,' Charlie said. 'What we're gonna do – is ter go back ter the mess and get some whisky and then we're gonna get them girls.'

'Where we getting the whisky from, Charlie?'

'I'll show yer,' he said.

They broke into the officers' mess. The corporal-cook, who had a room up above, came down and started shouting. Somebody hit him over the head with one of his own ladles, and he went out like a light. They could not break into the cellar, and contented themselves with what they could find behind the bar. It was after they had finished these that Charlie suggested they should fetch their rifles from the billets.

'All right,' he bellowed. 'Get yer skates on and be back in ten minutes' time.' Only half the men came back.

They circled the Town Guard-House – a former villa set well back in its own grounds – like the old hands they were in spite of their drunkenness. They accounted for the sentry at the gate, and a moment later Charlie appeared, grinning.

'I've nobbled the prowler guard,' he said. 'It's all ours now.'

Jimmie pressed his hands firmly against the stock of his rifle. He wondered why he was tagging along with the others. He was not that drunk that he could not realize what they were letting themselves in for. You're with them because you belong with them, he told himself. Because you belong with them. They're your kind.

'Right,' Charlie whispered in the darkness. 'Let's get on with it.'

Jimmie moved forward with the rest. This is about the only thing you can be certain about, he thought, holding the rifle at the port across his body. The bushes and the long grass were wet with dew. You can be killed and kill. Just like the old days. Christ, the old days! It's only three months ago. It was then that the burst of automatic fire hit him squarely in the chest. Only three months ago, he was thinking, as he fell into the long, wet grass.

All around him the others were running heavily through the garden towards the wall. In the house the lights were going on. Somewhere he could hear someone shouting hoarsely:

'Haul yer butt out o' that pit, Murphy! Haul yer butt out o' that pit, Murphy!'

He could hear people approaching. A ring of faces peered down at him. An excited young voice kept saying:

'I didn't mean to hit him, sir. Honest I didn't! I didn't mean to hit him, sir!'

Christ, Jimmie thought. Only three months ago.

'Accidentally killed,' it said in the telegram.

'That means I get a pension, don't it?' she asked anxiously at the post office that Friday when she went up to collect her allowance. They told her she would, and Jimmie's wife went away a happy woman.

A few weeks later, near the end of the month, they sent his things. There was a cheap photograph of the two of them at Saltburn, taken that Sunday long ago.

'Bloody thing,' she murmured to herself, and tossed it to one side.

There were a few Belgian francs, a couple of German officer's hat badges, a crumpled picture of Jimmie's platoon, with the name of each man printed neatly in ink over his head. There was a heap of papers scribbled on in pencil. They were held together with a clip, and on the top page somebody had printed in pencil: 'The boy from Hope Street.'

'We used to live in Hope Street,' she mused aloud. At that moment she heard Frank shouting – 'her fancy man', as the neighbours called him – and with a gesture she threw the papers into the fire. 'Stupid bugger!'

The Regiment marched to the station, heads sunk down in their gas-capes. They carried their rifles reversed with the muzzles peeping out from underneath their capes. They had borrowed a band from the in-coming regiment – which had arrived fresh from England – and as the band played the Regimental March, the colonel took the salute in the pouring rain. He wore no over-coat, so that everyone could see his medal ribbons. As long as they could remember, they had never seen him wear a greatcoat.

'Eyes right! Eyes front!' They marched on sullenly under the heavy load of equipment they carried on their backs through the deserted glistening streets, their hobnails grating and sometimes striking sparks on the cobbles.

The band struck up 'Colonel Bogie' and someone began to sing the vulgar version of the march: 'Where was the engine-driver when the boiler bust? They found his...'

But nobody joined in and the song petered away. A lean black dog had joined the column, loping effortless at its side. An officer stepped out of the ranks to drive it away.

They disappeared into the distance and the noise of the band grew fainter and fainter. You could no longer hear the ring of the hobnails on the cobbles, and the officer was still trying to drive away the animal which dogged the column.

CLAUSEN

He hated the thought that anyone might see him, so he waited until it was quite dark before he began his search of the dust-bins. He had debated the idea with himself all day: should he or should he not search the dust-bins?

In a way, he was relieved when he found nothing. My common sense should have told me, he told himself, that people these days would have nothing to put in dust-bins.

It started to rain, and he turned up the collar of his jacket. He had sold his overcoat the week before for two loaves of bread and sixty cigarettes. He wished he had hung on to his coat. He wished he... His stomach rumbled noisily.

The rain started to come down in sheets, but he walked on, not seeming to notice. As he walked, he could feel the rain penetrating the hole in his sole. His shoes felt like tight wet cardboard, and he curled his foot up in his left shoe in a vain attempt to keep the foot dry.

He considered where he could sleep that night. He could not go to the bunker or the railway-station waiting-room – and it was becoming increasingly dangerous to sleep in the ruins; there had already been ten accidents from collapsing buildings this week, he'd heard that day. No, it would have to be under the bridge again, he decided. He had discovered the bridge two nights before. It ran over a disused canal and housed men like himself, who were afraid to sleep in public places or who were on the run.

When he reached the bridge, he was soaked to the skin, but that did not bother him. Already, one or two of the men had bedded themselves down on the sandy floor underneath the bridge, their arms and legs covered with sacks and newspapers, and their heads resting on rucksacks. He nodded to an old man holding a candle, whom he recognized from the night before, and sat down with his back against the ice-cold wall.

In the corner, an old man with a long, ragged beard and battered hat took out a piece of grey bread and began to eat it slowly. The other men under the bridge turned their eyes in his direction and watched him eat. When he had finished, and had taken a swig of water out of an army water-bottle, they let their eyes drop again. The man with the lighted candle drew the flame along the seams of his tattered shirt, killing the lice, and then blew it out. It was dark, and the men lay back and tried to sleep. Clausen could feel his clothes clinging to him – against his back where it pressed up along the wall, weighing heavy on the knees and tight between the crotch.

The old man who had eaten the bread came and lay down beside him with a grunt. Soon he fell asleep, but kept coughing and groaning. Once he started up and shouted aloud:

'Martha, I didn't want to! I didn't want to!'

Afterwards, Clausen could feel his heart beating rapidly from the shock. Somebody at the end of the bridge belched loudly. Eventually, Clausen fell asleep.

He was awakened by someone lying down beside him. He was about to say something when he realized that it was a woman. He lay very still and looked at the night sky. It was pitch black, with here and there a star twinkling very far away. He wondered stupidly why on some nights the stars seemed positively to light the whole sky up, and on others you couldn't see a star. He concluded it might be something to do with visibility. Probably he would have fallen asleep again there and then, if the woman next to him had not suddenly sprung up and rushed from under the bridge. He could hear her being sick, gulping air in noisily.

When she came back and lay down again, he could smell the cloying odour of vomit. Then she began to cry softly. Clausen waited for a moment, and then, touching her gently with his hand, he whispered:

'What's the matter, Fraulein?'

The woman did not answer, but stopped crying suddenly.

'Tell me,' he persisted.

'I'm going to have a baby,' she said in a hushed tone after a moment.

'That's not so bad. You don't need to cry about that.'

'There's no father,' she said baldly.

'Oh.'

Outside it began to rain again. They could hear the rain beat down noisily against the earth and run in hundreds of tiny streams down to the canal. The air grew noticeably colder. She moved closer to him for warmth, and he put his arm round her and pressed her tightly to him.

The other men stirred and turned uneasily in their sleep, except for the old man who lay next to Clausen. He's fallen off nicely,

Clausen thought enviously, as he felt the inert body next to him. The wind began to lash the rain underneath the bridge, and he spread the wet papers over the girl, who had no other covering than an old piece of sacking.

The girls' teeth chattered. 'I'm so terribly cold,' she said painfully. 'I think ... I'm going to die.'

'Don't be silly,' he said. He tried to say the words in a hearty tone, but all he could force out was a hoarse croak. 'Where ... are you ... cold?'

'My legs ... and ... feet,' she whispered slowly.

He lifted the sheets of paper and began laboriously to rub her feet and legs between his stiff fingers. She pressed herself closer to him.

'Is that any ... better?' he asked grimly, breathing heavily as if he had run a race.

'A bit,' she said weakly, 'but I'm so cold ... so cold. Oh, I'm going to die... I'm going to die.'

'You're not going to die,' he said grimly. A kind of anger at the rain and the cold and the bridge was growing within him.

Painfully, he forced himself round and faced her...

When they woke again, it was morning, and already most of the other men were awake and getting ready to start their daily search of the dust-bins and gutters. Every bone of Clausen's body seemed stiff, and he could not feel his feet at all. He lay there for a moment and looked at the dull, grey-streaked morning sky. God, what a night, he thought, and rubbed his unshaven chin reflectively.

It had stopped raining, and the birds seemed to be making a terrible noise. He got to his feet stiffly like an old man and rubbed the white scum from his lips. Then he began to slap his hands vigorously across his body to get warm. Everyone had gone now except the old man, who still slept on under his cover of wet newspapers.

He woke the girl. She stared up at him, as if he really did not exist. 'Is it morning?' she asked, and shivered.

Her remark suddenly seemed terribly funny to him, and he laughed thickly. She looked at him, puzzled, and he said:

'Yes.'

He held out his hand and pulled her to her feet.

'How do you feel this morning?' he said.

'Cold.'

This, too, seemed to him tremendously funny, but he restrained himself. Her dress was crumpled and stained, and he could see now that she was pregnant.

'Who's the father?' he asked.

She shrugged her shoulders. 'I don't know. There have been many in the last months.'

He changed the subject.

'Let's wake the old man,' he said, 'and get on our way.'

He bent down and shook the old man by the shoulder.

'Come on, old man. Wake up. The sun will be blinding you soon.'

The old man did not make a move. Clausen looked puzzled, and then tried again.

'Come on, old one. This is not place to lie abed.'

Still the old man did not move. Clausen bent down and looked closely at the old man. Then he felt his pulse and stood up slowly. He looked hard at the girl.

'The old one's dead,' he said slowly. 'Must have died during the night. I remember him coughing a bit ... and then all of a sudden he went very quiet during the night. It must have been then...' He spoke, as if to himself.

The girl did not say anything, but looked at the grey face of the dead man, his lips drawn back to reveal yellow, decayed teeth. Clausen bent down and took the rucksack from beneath his head. He opened it and rummaged among its contents for a moment. Then he took out a cloth bundle from which he drew a crust of grey bread. He broke it in two and gave a piece to the girl.

'I knew he had another bit somewhere,' he said, in explanation.

The girl took a bite, and rushed from under the bridge to vomit. She came back and ate the rest.

'We did it there – and he was already dead,' she said slowly, as if in a dream. 'Stretched out dead beside us.'

He tried to put his hand on her arm to comfort her, but she drew back, her eyes fixed on the dead man's face.

After a moment, they got up and left the dead man among the old sacks and wet newspapers, his face covered by an old bit of sacking. They walked down the deserted road between the ruins. The sun came out weakly and warmed their chilled bones.

'So you're called Ilka, and you're going to have a baby…' he began kindly.

'We did it and he was dead beside us.'

A black dog which had been nuzzling in the gutter turned and stared at them as they passed. Then it left whatever it had been doing and began to pad after them silently.

And the little girl, who was going to die that winter, wrote in her exercise-book:

'A little boy and a girl were sitting at the sea-side. And the little boy and girl made a sand-castle. And the waves came up and washed it away. And one day they went on a big ship. And when they got out to sea there was a storm. And they could all swim. And they all got back to the shore. And when they got home all the land was bombed and there were some more bombs. And so all the people were killed and the men in the aeroplanes laughed.'

The publishers hope that this book has given you enjoyable reading. Large Print Books are especially designed to be as easy to see and hold as possible. If you wish a complete list of our books please ask at your local library or write directly to:

Dales Large Print Books
Magna House, Long Preston,
Skipton, North Yorkshire.
BD23 4ND

This Large Print Book, for people
who cannot read normal print,
is published under the auspices of

THE ULVERSCROFT FOUNDATION